T0368163

ACES HIGH

JEANETTE KOSSUTH MCADOO

authorHOUSE

AuthorHouse™
1663 Liberty Drive
Bloomington, IN 47403
www.authorhouse.com
Phone: 1 (800) 839-8640

Published by AuthorHouse 08/27/2019

ISBN: 978-1-7283-2048-9 (sc)
ISBN: 978-1-7283-2047-2 (e)

Print information available on the last page.

This book is printed on acid-free paper.

I dedicate this book to four people who inspired this novel: Autumn Snyder, Ronnie Snyder, Logan Evagues and Noah Evagues. Thank you.

Also I would like to thank my son, Timothy V. Rump. He has always been my pillar of strength, he encourages me and is always there for me. I love you and couldn't be more proud. Mom

IN MEMORIAN OF RONALD A. SNYDER July 28, 1967 ~ May 30, 2019

Ronald Snyder, husband of Kimberly Oelschalger, father of Ronnie and Autumn Snyder, Uncle of Logan and Noah Evagues

Chapter 1

The funeral was over, Logan, Noah, Ronnie and Autumn sat in the kitchen drinking coffee and feeling numb. Logan and Noah traveled from Anaconda Montana to attend the funeral of their Aunt Kim and Uncle Ron, Autumn and Ronnie's parents. It was just last year when they lost their parents, Patti and Ron, in a stagecoach accident. Only Kim and Ron were brutally murdered and for no apparent reason. Noah was a bounty hunter and Logan has his practice as a doctor. Though they were close, not even living in two states could ever split them. Noah saw the pain in Autumn's eyes.

> "Autumn, Ronnie I promise you both I will find who did this, I won't stop till I do."

Noah is the best and well known bounty hunter in Montana. He's never failed a hunt yet. Ronnie looked over to him.

> "I know you will, thank you."

Autumn hasn't talked much since this happened, Ronnie didn't know what to do for her. She poured more coffee for everyone and just kept busy constantly. Logan took her hand and spoke.

> "We're all family, we need to be together now. I know it will be difficult but why don't you both think of moving to Anaconda and be near us, I think the change will be good for both of you."

Ronnie glanced at Autumn before he spoke.

> "Thank you Logan but I don't think..."

Autumn broke in the conversation.
> "I think it's a great idea, we need a fresh start. I can't stay here and live in this house with a memory of what happened."

Ronnie was astonished at her decision, he never thought she would ever want to leave this house. All though her reason for leaving is a good one. How could they stay after what happened?

> "Autumn are you sure?"

Ronnie couldn't figure her out right now, but in time she would be fine.

> "I'm very sure."

They all looked at each other then Logan spoke.

> "Sounds like it's all settled to me. Is there anything we can do to help?"

Ronnie shook his head and explained there isn't much and they would be along as soon as things are finished. Ronnie knew of someone who wanted to buy the house and they didn't have much to pack.

> "Autumn and I will be fine. I know you two have things you need to tend to back home, I'll send you a wire when we're ready to leave."

There was silence, Autumn was just keeping busy moving around the kitchen cleaning up whether it needed done or not. They all understood her actions.

> "Well... Noah and I will be heading back, we hope to see you again soon."

Both Noah and Logan hugged Autumn telling her the hurt will pass and how much easier it will be for them all to be together. Ronnie walked them to the door said their good byes, then turned to Autumn wishing he knew what to do for her. Their father was the town's blacksmith and their mother a seamstress. Everyone loved them, what possible reason could there be for wanting them dead?

> "You know this is a good thing Autumn, we can all be a family again. We will get through this I promise. I'm going out to check on the horses, I won't be long."

Ronnie knew she heard him, he didn't say anymore, he just walked out to the stable. Autumn's attention was caught by a picture of the family together last Christmas. Who would have thought it would be their last Christmas together. It was the best one yet. Autumn and Kim baked, Ronnie and Ron cut down the tree to decorate and he taught Ronnie how to make the Christmas punch. Autumn could almost smell the aroma from her and her mother baking. Their parents would wrap presents after Ronnie and Autumn were in bed. Friends dropped in and they songs together and shared food and punch. They went to church and came home and enjoyed the day just being together.

Autumn packed the picture in her bag then went to bed. This whole ordeal was horrendous, Ronnie would most likely turn in as well. When he did come in he could hear Autumn crying, he pretended he couldn't hear her to give her time to herself. They would always be there for each other no matter what. It was nearly an hour later when Autumn finally went to sleep. Ronnie lay in bed wide awake, how could he sleep knowing what took place here, it just wasn't right. The night was long, Ronnie glanced out the window at the starry filled sky. A captivating night possessing an extravagant moon, the kind of night his mother enjoyed. Before long he drifted off to sleep. The night was quiet when a few hours later Autumn woke up screaming, Ronnie rushed to her side and held her tight.

"It's ok I'm here."

She was shaking as he held her, letting her release her frustrations.

"You just had a bad dream. That's all it was."

She was terrified, it wasn't long before she went back to sleep, Ronnie lay her down gently and pulled the blanket up to her shoulders then he kissed her on her forehead.

"It'll take time but we will be fine. I promise."

He went back to bed and was back to sleep. The remaining of that night flew by and Ronnie woke up to the aroma of breakfast.

"Do I smell pancakes and bacon?"

She turned and told him to have a seat, she was about to serve.

"Yes you do, blueberry, your favorite. Coffee coming right up."

She sat down to have breakfast with him.

"With so much to do I thought you could use a big breakfast."

However his plans differed from hers.

"I'm going to send you ahead by train, pack your things and I'll take you into town."

"No, you can't travel alone, I'm going with you."

They both were hard headed.

"There's nothing here I need you for, wrapping things up won't take long and no trouble. You'd be better off in Anaconda. I'll be along soon enough and that's it, no arguments."

"You can't travel alone."

This was not going to be easy.

"I can and I will. It's no way for you to travel. Besides you can get
things set up for us, now that's that."

Not that she would admit to him but he was right. After breakfast she cleaned up and
packed her bags and started packing some of what she could for Ronnie to put on the wagon.
He rode her into town an bought a ticket for the train and waited to see her off.

"Before you go I found this last night. It's mother's locket that we gave
her for her birthday, you should have this."

Autumn was nearly in tears.

"I looked all over for this. I thought it was gone forever."

He put the locket on her just before she boarded the train.

"I found it on the floor next to their bed. She must have dropped it and
didn't realize it was missing."

She was so happy to have the locket she didn't care where he found it. Just that he did.

"Take care and be careful Ronnie, I'll see you in Montana."

"I will, I'm going to send a wire to Logan right now. Be safe."

She went to her compartment and sat down staring out the window and waving good bye
to her brother. The train pulled out and when Ronnie could see her no more he went to send
a wire to Logan and Noah. As he was leaving the office a little boy who always hung around
Ronnie came up to him.

"Mr. Ronnie, I have something for you. My Paw helped me make it,
it's a hedgehog. Paw carved it for me and I put it on the key chain. It's
to keep you safe and bring you good luck."

Ronnie took the keychain from Billy admiring it, he and Billy had a special relationship.
His father was always busy trying to keep the family fed. They lead a hard life and Ronnie
always did what he could to help. He picked up Billy and hugged him.

"Thank you Billy, I'll always keep it with me. Now you be good and
help your Paw all right? I promise I'll come back to see you."

Billy hugged him so tight tears ran down his face.

"I'll miss you Mr. Ronnie."

Ronnie knew he would miss Billy, but things had to be this way.

"When I come back to see you I'll bring you a special present. How does that sound? You'll always be my best buddy. Now you go on, your Paw may need you, I'll see you when I come back. I'll even send you a post card after I get there, with pictures of Montana."

"Really? Thank you, thank you a whole lot."

Billy gave Ronnie one last hug then ran home to help his father. Ronnie rode over to see Mr. Porter about selling him the house. For what ever reason that house seemed very important to him, he never pressured to buy it, just if they would ever sell it he would want to buy.

"Hello Mr. Porter, how are you today?"

He saw Ronnie and stood up to welcome him.

"Hi Ronnie, you know the whole town will miss your parents. Darned shame what happen, can't imagine why. You know everyone in town loved your folks. So what brings you here today?"

Ronnie had a lump in his throat. What he had to do wasn't easy.

"Mr Porter, are you still interested in buying my parents house?"

Bart looked puzzled, for years he's been wanting to buy that house.

"Well sure am. Mind if I ask why you'd want to sell?"

"My sister and I are moving, we just can't stay in that house. Of course if you don't want to buy it I'll surely understand."

He looked at Ronnie knowing how difficult this was for him.

"Son, I am still interested and I promise I'll take good care of it, the way your parents did. You know your father and I built that house before you were born. I'm sorry your selling it, but I understand."

"Thank you sir, if you want to come out to the house this afternoon. I'll have the papers and we can sign them. Then it's all yours."

He agreed to meet Ronnie then said he would see him there as Ronnie turned and walked away. Hopping up on the wagon and heading back to the house Ronnie took his time, he wanted to enjoy Cheyenne as much as he could before he moved. There were so many great times for him and his family. At least the good memories was something he could take with him. Along the way he passed a fishing hole where he and his father used to fish. What ever they caught they would bring home for dinner. An apple tree where he and Autumn, as young kids would climb and eat apples.

Now they start over with their cousins and begin a new life. It wouldn't be easy at first but hard work and time, they will make it again. When Ronnie arrived back at the house he went inside to pack. Nothing much just what they needed,or things they wanted. Then he went to the stables to feed the horses, all but two would stay. He knew Mr. Porter would take good care of them. On the porch were wind chimes he made for his mother, she loved them. Those would most definitely go with him. Soon he had the wagon packed with everything they wanted, then he looked up and saw Mr. Porter headed his way, time to finalize the sale.

> "Hello, is it afternoon all ready? I've been so busy I haven't paid much attention to the time."

Mr. Porter smiled.

> "I could come back if you need more time."

> "No no you're fine, just lost track is all. Come on inside."

They went inside and he handed Ronnie an envelope.

> "This is too generous, I can't take all this money."

> "Yes you can. You and your sister are starting over, you'll need every cent you can get. Besides I think that's a bargain. Take it, use it to start your new life."

Ronnie was taught never to argue with his elders, also he didn't want to admit they could use the money. He thanked Bart then said good bye. They shook hands and Ronnie was on his way.

In Anaconda Noah picked up the wire sent to him. He rushed over to show it to Logan.

> "Well they're coming. Ronnie sent Autumn on a train, she will be here the day after tomorrow then he'll follow. He's traveling by wagon so it will take him a day or two more but we'll all be together again."

They smiled and couldn't wait for them both to arrive.

6

"You know what I was thinking? Remember when we were younger? Autumn used to talk about owning her own business."

"That's right I remember, but you think she'll still want to? That was a long time ago."

Nodding his head he was sure Autumn would still want her own business.

"Well I talked to Marsha Dawson and she is selling her saloon. Her mother took ill and she needs to go back to Texas to run the ranch for her. It would be perfect for Autumn, she could live in the upstairs room and still run the business all in the same building, like Marsha did."

Noah smiled knowing that would be great for her, and Ronnie could stay at his place, he was hardly ever home anyway.

"Sounds great except for one thing, Autumn doesn't have the money. Too bad, something like this could be good for her, keep her busy."

Logan agreed with Noah, this could be just the thing, great therapy.

"Well don't forget, Ronnie sold the house and they will split what they make on that. Besides if it isn't enough I can lend her what she may need. Being there for each other is what family is all about. May even help her to recover from this tragedy."

Noah was thinking, you could always tell by the expression on his face.

"Ronnie is traveling by himself, I hope he'll be all right without anyone with him."

Ronnie learned a lot from Noah and his father, he could handle any situation. He had traveled a little ways when he came to a lake, there was a huge boulder near there. Suddenly he heard a scream. He jumped off the wagon and followed the scream. An Indian woman was being attacked by a white man. Ronnie pulled out his gun and shot it in the air.

"Leave her alone and step back, now."

The man just looked at him and stepped back, then he spoke.

"Why are you defending her, she's just a dirty old squaw?"

That was all Ronnie needed. He dropped his gun then went over with his fist and the man fell to the ground.

> "I don't like your kind, get out of here before I finish this. You won't come out alive if I do that's a promise."

The man stood up and got on his horse. He took one last look at the Indian woman.

> "May as well, she's not worth it anyway."

With that he rode off before Ronnie could do any more. He helped the woman up to her feet to make sure she was all right. He noticed her dress was torn.

> "Let me fix that, we don't want you going around with a torn dress. I'm Ronnie, and what is your name?"

She looked at him gratefully that he helped her.

> "My name is Chanda, it means the moon. I was born when the moon was full."

> "That's very nice, I like that."

Ronnie was sitting with her and mending her dress.

> "Thank you for helping me. I don't know what I would have done if you hadn't come along when you did."

Ronnie looked a her and smiled.

> "I'm glad I came along too, you're safe now. Let me take you back to your tribe. What are you doing here by yourself anyway?"

She went to fill her pails with water before she returned.

> "I was sent to fill these pails."

> "Well maybe you shouldn't come alone anymore, for your own safety. Next time there may not be anyone around."

She smiled and was grateful. Ronnie helped her with the pails and put them in the wagon then helped her up. Chanda guided him to her tribe, it wasn't very far. When they arrived she told her father what happened and how Ronnie saved her. Chandra's father was the tribes chief.

"Ronnie, this is my father, Chief Achak. His name means spirit. Father this is Ronnie, he saved me from a man who tried to hurt me."

Her father said to her, apane tepe ke jao. Ronnie was not sure what happened but he spoke to him.

"I hope I did nothing to cause her trouble, I just tried to help her."

The chief stared at him a moment then spoke.

"I just told her to go to her tee-pee. Thank you for your help. I would like you to stay and smoke the peace pipe with me. You are a friend of our tribe. Please."

Ronnie couldn't refuse and agreed.

"I can stay a while but I must keep moving."

Chief Achak had Chandra set up for the ceremony. It was his way of welcoming Ronnie to the tribe and make him their friend. The chief sat across from Ronnie and began the ritual. Chandra would explain to Ronnie as her father began.

"First he beseeches the west presenting the spirit world, then the north which is the source of endurance, strength and truthfulness. Next the east where the sun rises and brings us knowledge. Finally the south bringing a bounty of medicine and growth. Then the pipe is touched to the ground and he speaks the words: Mother earth I seek to protect you. Then the pipe is held to the sky, the great spirit of mystery and explainable source of life. Again he speaks: Oh great spirit, thank you for the six powers of the universe. Now you will smoke."

The chief begins by puffing several times then hands the pipe to Ronnie. He then hands the pipe back to the chief.

"You are now a friend of the Blackfoot tribe. If you ever need anything, we're here for you."

Ronnie thanked him but he had to move on. Chandra kissed him on the cheek and they watched as he rode away. Ronnie stopped the wagon and looked back once more to wave good bye. He had to keep moving if he was going to make it to Anaconda when he said he would. Autumn was in good hands, he knew that. Maybe even Logan could help her get through whatever it is she's suppressing.

While traveling all the way he has so far Ronnie has had time to think, think about a new start, his old life before all this happened, his heart still hurting. Like he told Autumn that will pass, but for now it didn't seem like it ever would. He was the man now and had to take care not only of Autumn but himself. At least he has time to clear his head and enjoy the beautiful scenery. Smoking a peace pipe with the Indians was an experience he'll never forget. He's been traveling for a few hours now and it is getting close to supper time. Just then one of the horses whinnied and stopped moving. The horse kept whinnying and jumping up and down in one place. Ronnie jumped down to check on the horse.

"What's wrong boy? Take it easy, take it easy."

He saw the horse was holding his front leg up, when Ronnie checked his hoof he found a pebble wedged in, Ronnie took out his pocket knife and pulled it out.

"OK fella it's fine now. I think we need a rest anyway."

Ronnie grabbed the feeding bags from the back of the wagon for the horses. While they were eating Ronnie cooked some chili over a camp fire, like his father taught him how to make it when they went hunting together. There was a creek nearby, after the horses ate he took them to the creek for a drink and brought back some water for coffee and cooking. Somehow cooking over a campfire smelled so good, even the coffee. The sun was beginning to set and darkness grew in the sky.

"Well fellas I think we're setting up camp here. We'll get an early start in the morning while it's cooler. It will be better for both of us."

Ronnie cleaned up and sat by the fire till it died out, then turned in for the night. The sky was clear and filled with stars, and all Ronnie could think about was Autumn and his cousins.

The next morning in Anaconda Logan went to talk to Marsha about buying her saloon for Autumn.

"Marsha you know we'll miss you. No one any where could ever take your place and we sure are sorry to hear about your mother."

Marsha knew everyone in town, they were all like family.

"I'll miss everyone too but there's nothing I can do. As soon as I sell this place I'm gone. Sooner I hope, my mother really needs me."

Logan understood and hugged Marsha letting her know how sorry everyone is to hear about her mother taking ill.

"Marsha your saloon is what I wanted to talk to you about. My cousin Autumn is arriving tomorrow. I told you about my cousin's parent's. Well since she was little she wanted to have her own establishment. With all that's happened I thought this place would be great for her. Keep her busy you know?"

Marsha knew exactly what he meant.

"If she's anything like you and Noah she'll be right for my saloon. I'd be happy to sell it to her."

"Well that's the other thing. I'd like to buy it for her as a surprise when she arrives. If you don't have a problem with that?"

"No problem what so ever. Come on, I'll buy you a drink then we can sign the papers."

Logan was excited for Autumn.

"Coffee will be fine, I have to see patients today. Thank you." Together they went inside to take care of things. Not long after Noah came in looking for Logan.

"Logan your needed at the office. I brought in Mrs. James, she went into labor and that baby isn't waiting. You need to come quick."

Everything was settled and Logan thanked Marsha for everything promising to talk with her later. The brothers rushed out the door and over to the office to check on Mrs. James. Noah stood behind her while Logan checked her and prepared to deliver her baby. Noah held her hands and she squeezed them so tight when she screamed in pain. Soon Logan delivered a healthy baby boy. Noah left her in Logan's capable hands and went to find her husband.

"Sam is working in the mines, please hurry."

Mrs. James was exhausted from the delivery, Logan let her hold her baby till her husband arrived to take her home and get some much needed rest, he made her as comfortable as possible.

"Thank you so much doctor, I didn't know what I would have done if Noah hadn't happened by. I was frightened."

"Everything is fine now, Sam should be here any minute. Just relax."

Marsha walked in and Logan heard the bell hanging from the door going out to the waiting room. There was Marsha.

"I saw Noah leaving, if it's all right may I see Linda and the baby?"

He nodded and let her in the room, it was good for Linda to have someone with her until her Sam got there. A little female company could do her some good. Logan was filling out paper work for his files when his first appointment walked in, Logan pointed to the room for him to go till he finished the paperwork. Just as he was filing them, Noah came in with Sam.

"Where is she doc? Is she okay?"

"Go on in and see for yourself."

Sam was jittery and excited at the same time. He combed his hair and straightened his shirt then walked in with a smile in his face, the proud father. Marsha walked out to leave them alone and give them time together.

"They're naming the baby Wyatt James. Thank you for letting me visit with her. I'll be going home to an ailing mother and it's nice to be a part of a joyous event. I needed that." Noah walked over to hug her.

"Marsha Dawson we'll miss you, but we send you with prays. If there is anything we can do, please let us know. You're still family to us, even in Texas."

"Yes I will, as much as I'll miss everyone here. I do appreciate everyone here in this town. Like you said we're all like family and I'll miss that more than anything."

With that being said Marsha had things to take care of and was on her way back to the saloon. Sam came out of the room with his wife and baby thanking both Noah and Logan for all they did and invited them to dinner one night after all has settled.

Meanwhile Marsha wanted to do one last thing before she left town, so she talked to some of the women to get together and take things over to the James's house for the baby and mother. Marsha had been working on a quilt for the baby when Linda first told people she was going to have a baby. Some of the other women had gifts for mother and baby, they were all excited to have this little party for the family. That evening around supper time Marsha had cooked a meal for the family, with a new baby they probably never even thought about food.

Marsha had cooked and taken over a steak dinner for the new mother and father. She walked over to their house and knocked on the door.

"Miss Dawson, what a surprise! What brings you here."

Sam noticed she was carrying a big basket.

"Well with a new baby I thought you may have forgotten about supper. So I cooked a steak dinner to celebrate your new baby."

Sam was so pleased, he took the basket from her and invited her inside.

"Well my gosh is it time for supper all ready? I guess your right, we didn't think about that. How can we ever thank you? Why don't you sit down and join us?"

She smiled and shook her head no.

"Thank you but this is a celebration for you and Linda. The two of you should have this time for yourselves. Enjoy and I'll stop by tomorrow to check on things. Have a good night."

"Thank you again Marsha, oh and we're awful sorry about your mother taking ill like she has. We'll be praying for you both."

"Thank you."

Marsha left and went back to the saloon and up to her room. There was packing to get done among other things to tidy up, in a couple of days she was heading back to Texas. Tomorrow she and the other women were planning to stop by the James's house to give them gifts for the new born. A baby was always a blessed and a special event, the town's women did what they could to help the new parents any way they could.

Logan stopped at Noah's house for some coffee and conversation. Tomorrow Autumn will arrive and the brothers would meet her at the station, Logan couldn't wait to tell Autumn about the saloon, Noah had a room ready for Ronnie when he finally made it to town.

"Logan, you don't reckon we're jumping the gun about Autumn do you? I mean it feels like we're planning her life for her."

"No that's not it at all. We're just trying to help her move on with her life. She'll never forget her parents and neither will Ronnie. Do you remember what we went through?"

Noah thought about what was said, remembering how things were when they lost their parents. Besides Autumn doesn't have to run the saloon. She can make her decision after she arrives.

> "You're right, all we're trying to do is help them through this. They didn't have to move here, they could have stayed in Cheyenne and lived in another house. Found their way again there, but now we'll have family again and so will they."

Logan stood up and said good night.

> "I'll see you in the morning and we'll meet Autumn when her train comes in, everything will work out fine. Relax."

Noah went inside to turn in for the night but could barely sleep he was so excited. Things may get off to a slow start but once it does they will smooth out and everything will be great again. It will just take some time. Autumn may need some extra care, she was really in a bad way. Of course anyone who this happened to would be but it was something more with her. No one could figure it out and pressuring her may only make things worse. Maybe Logan could do something for her. Maybe he all ready has by buying the saloon.

The next morning they were at the train station waiting to meet their cousin. When the train pulled in they waited to see Autumn. Passengers were stepping down but they didn't see her. A woman walked up behind them and she spoke.

> "Are you looking for someone?"

It was Autumn, they hugged each other then they went to Noah's house to talk and have coffee. She seemed a little bit better but not by much, even a little was better than not. Logan set his cup down and looked at her.

> "I have a surprise for you, come with me there is someone I want you to meet."

They walked over to the saloon and he introduced her to Marsha.

> "Hello, welcome to Anaconda. Your cousin has told me so much about you.'

Autumn had a blank look on her face. Then Logan explained.

> "Remember when we were kids and you use to talk about having your own business?"

"Yes I do, I don't think that will ever happen." Marsha and Logan looked at each other and smiled.

"It just has. Marsha sold this place, her mother took ill and she has to move to Texas to tend to her mother's ranch. I bought this place for you."

Autumn was astonished, she didn't know what to say.

"I can't let you buy me this place."

"I all ready did, you can pay me back when you can, no hurry."

She was about ready to cry.

"I'll leave you here with Marsha and you two can talk about the whole thing. She'll show you everything, really it isn't that hard. You're a very bright young woman, you'll learn this in no time."

With that being said Logan left the two of them to go over the details. Now all they needed was Ronnie and something for him. Logan was sure it would happen for him, they couldn't wait for him to get in town.

During Ronnie's travels things were going along fine when a wheel cracked and the wagon tipped over, Ronnie was lucky, he was thrown a short distance. Other wise he may have been caught underneath and trapped. He unhooked the horses and tied them to a nearby tree until he could fix the wheel and somehow get the wagon turned upright again. There was a clap of thunder, he had to work fast. There wasn't much to unload then he could use the horses to upturn the wagon. Thunder was cracking and the sky grew an ugly dark. He hooked up the horses to the side of the wagon.

"Sorry fellas but...Pull!"

The horses started moving but it was rough. Ronnie kept repeating pull and after a few more times the wagon upturned.

"Whoa boys, take it easy. Good job fellas."

Ronnie petted them and looked back. This would be a delay for sure, he couldn't fix the wheel in the rain. Ronnie looked up and saw a huge lightening bolt. In the not too far distance he saw an abandoned barn. Judging from the pile of rubble almost next to the barn it would seem a house burned down.

> "Well boys, the wagon has to stay here but we'll go and stay in that barn till this weather passes."

Ronnie pulled out a couple of trunks from the wagon to hold it in place so it wouldn't tip over then unhooked the horses and went to the barn. Just as he opened the barn doors it began to pour.

> "Good thank you for all your blessings on this trip and thank you for this barn. I know you're watching over us."

There was nothing more that could be done for now. Ronnie pulled three apples from his sack, one for him and one for each horse.

> "You boys are working hard this trip and I'm grateful. I think you both deserve a treat, here have an apple."

Then he sat down to enjoy his apple and watched the rain fall. Ronnie pulled out a candle to have a look around. There hanging on the wall was a wagon wheel.

> "Well boys God is looking out for us, who ever lived here left everything behind. Look at this, a wagon wheel."

One man's tragedy is another mans blessing, that was the only way to look at this. Ronnie took the candle and walked around to see if there was anything else he could make use of, it' a shame to just leave things like this. He found a sack of horse feed he could make use of and a few tools. There was a noise outside and Ronnie picked up a pitch fork and slowly walked to the entrance. He raised the pitch fork ready to use it if he had to when he heard a gun click.

> "That's right cowboy, I'm here to settle a score with you. You need to learn how to mind your own business."

Ronnie recognized him as the man who attacked Chandra, the Indian woman.

> "When an innocent man or woman is being attacked I make it my business."

> "Well now you'll have pay cowboy."

The man had a strange look on his face, then he hit the ground. There was an arrow in his back. An Indian man appeared.

"He came here to kill you. My sister Chandra saw him and asked me to follow. Good for you that I did. I'm Arjun."

"Well thank you, I'm really glad to meet you. So this guy holds a grudge pretty well I see?"

"He does. That was not the first attack he made on my sister. Only the law won't believe us because we're Indian."

Ronnie was upset, what kind of lawman let's this happen.

"Indian or not the law should have handled this."

Arjun believed his father when he was told Ronnie is a friend.

"Let me help you with your wagon, you can get back to your travels faster."

Ronnie agreed to let him help. He lost enough time as it is and needed to get to town to send a wire. It wasn't long before they had the wagon working again.

"This time I get to thank you. Your father, sister and you speak English very well."

"We picked it up, we had to for communication with the white man."

"Not all white men are like him, I know it's hard to trust."

Arjun nodded, they try to get along but they are labeled. It takes a long time to prove yourself.

"I will be back to visit, I hope your tribe may live in peace, and safety."

Arjun thanked him and wished him a safe trip.

"I will take care of things here, you go in peace, brother."

Ronnie smiled thanked him again then was on his way. The next town isn't far away so Ronnie could stop, send a wire and have some supper. The trip so far has been interesting, made an enemy, made some friends. He certainly had a lot to tell everyone back in Anaconda.

Straight ahead was the town, Ronnie could use a bit of a rest. When he rode into town he found a quiet, what seemed to be a friendly place. He rode his wagon to the livery stable then went to the telegraph office to send a wire, then went to the saloon for some supper. He was tired and decided to spend the night then start out again in the morning.

Autumn was sitting on the porch at Noah's house having a cup of coffee, she seemed worried. Noah came out to join her.

"Autumn, is something wrong?"

She looked up at Noah with great concern.

"Where is Ronnie? He should have been here by now? I knew he shouldn't have traveled by himself."

Noah was wondering the same thing but he didn't want to upset Autumn. He looked up and saw Logan coming their way.

"Hello you two, beautiful night isn't it, clear and the air is fresh."

Then he saw her face.

"Relax Autumn, I just received this wire from Ronnie. He said he was delayed and he'll explain everything when he gets here, tomorrow around supper time. In the meantime he is safe."

Autumn let out a sigh of relief. Noah had his arm around her.

"Well that is good to hear. Don't worry sweetie, he'll be fine."

"Well if you two will excuse me, I'm really tired. I'll see you both in the morning. Stop over I'll have breakfast ready."

They said good night and watched as Autumn went back to the saloon.

"Logan, I'm worried about her, she's really in a bad way."

"I know, we have to pay close attention to her. I can't pin it down but I feel like something inside is waiting to explode."

Autumn changed and ready to turn in, only she couldn't sleep. She was sure once she was in Anaconda things would start looking up even a little, but nothing. She couldn't understand what was happening. She lay in bed staring out the window, she could see the stars in the sky. Thoughts of happy times went through her head then suddenly she felt sleepy. Her eyes grew heavy and before long she was asleep. The night was quiet and peaceful.

Almost into the middle of the night there was a knock on her door, anxiously waiting for Autumn to answer.

"I'm coming, I'm coming." Marsha was at the door.

> "I'm sorry to wake you but we have an emergency. The orphanage caught fire and I need your help with the children. They need a place to sleep, will you help me please?"

> "Of course, let me throw something on and I'll be right down."

The orphanage on fire, it wasn't enough these children had no parents, now they lost their home, the only one they know. All this sadness at one time was too much. Autumn threw on a long shirt then went down to help Marsha. Children scared and crying, Marsha and Autumn had taken them upstairs to tuck them in for the night. There was one little girl who was so scared she couldn't stop crying. Autumn stayed with her. She talked to the little girl for a while then held her in her arms and sang a song her mother sang to her when she was little.

Marsha was watching them without Autumn realizing she was standing in the doorway. The song calmed the little girl then she looked up at Autumn.

> "I'm scared. What will happen to us?"

A question Autumn was familiar with herself.

> "Sweetheart, everything will be fine, it will just take some time. I promise."

Autumn tucked her in and stayed with her until she was in a deep sleep. Autumn went quietly downstairs to talk to Marsha.

> "What happened? How did it happen?"

Marsha looked at her wishing she cold tell her why.

> "Honey I just don't know. Logan and Noah and the men in town are all over there trying to put the fire out. Thank God no one was hurt. The children will have to stay here and the saloon will close for the time being, at least until we can figure out something."

> "I'll put on some coffee and make sandwiches to take to them, they'll be hungry I'm sure."

Marsha stayed with the children while Autumn took care of the food. The men came over a couple at a time for a quick break, had a sandwich and coffee then right back to put out the fire. After all the children were asleep Marsha came down to help. Logan and Noah came in, sat at a table and Autumn brought them food and coffee.

> "Are you both all right?"

She was concerned, she couldn't bare to lose more family.

> "We're fine, how are the children?'

Marsha came out from the kitchen.

> "They are fine, Autumn worked wonders with a very frightened little girl."

> "It was nothing, just a song my mother use to sing to me when I was little."

Then she started thinking about Ronnie.

> "Logan, you said Ronnie will be here by supper time tomorrow?"

> "That's what he said in his wire. He'll explain what the delay was about when he gets here."

What a welcome it will be when he does arrive. Leaving one tragedy and into another. At least this time no one was hurt, like Marsha said. These poor children, what will they do? One of the towns men came into the saloon.

> "I just wanted to let ya all know, the fire is out and tomorrow we start rebuilding, or the day after. Everyone is pitching in and in the meantime, some of the people will take children in with them until the new orphanage is rebuilt. Father Morgan set up beds at the church for the children so we will make sure every child has a place to stay."

Autumn was happy they would be taken care of, she offered to help anyway she could. The sun began to rise and the night was gone almost as quickly as it came. She and Marsha were exhausted, as soon as the children were placed the saloon remained closed and the two women went to their rooms to get some sleep.

Chapter 2

It was mid-morning and Father Morgan stopped by the saloon. Autumn was up and greeted him.

"Father Morgan, good morning. My name is Autumn, I'm Logan and Noah's cousin."

"Yes I heard a great deal about you, is your brother Ronnie here?"

"No not yet, he's traveling by wagon with our things. He sent a wire saying he should be here before supper. You're here for the children?"

"Yes I am. I understand some of the women will also be taking children in as well?"

"Yes they will."

Marsha was coming downstairs with a line of children following.

"Here they are Father, ready to go, Autumn fixed breakfast for them. She's been a great help through all of this." Father Morgan looked at her and smiled.

"My child I understand you have been through quit an ordeal yourself. You are a brave woman to help with all this after what you went through. May God bless you. We will talk soon."

Some of the towns women came in to take some of the children, no child will be left out, each one taken care of. The little girl who Autumn sang to walked up to her.

"Miss Autumn, will I see you again?"

"You will I promise, right now you go with Father Morgan. I'll stop by later to see you."

The little girl lifted her arms to hug Autumn, she really didn't want to leave her but she had to hoping she will see her again. She hugged her so tight Autumn thought she would never let go.

"I'll tell you what, what if later on I stop by the church, I'll take you out for a while and we can go shopping. How does that sound?"

The little girl was so happy and excited.

"Okay, oh and you can call me Sally."

"OK Sally, that's if it's ok with Father Morgan."

They both looked at him and he just couldn't say no. Sally seemed to be so attached to Autumn.

"I think that would be fine."

Autumn gave her one last hug and told Sally she would stop by later. Sally took Father Morgan's hand and went with him and the other children.

"You really made an impression on Sally, she really likes you."

"I really like her too, she's a great little girl."

Marsha saw the look in Autumn's eyes, there was no mistake, they were both attached to each other.

"Well I better get in the kitchen and get busy, there will be some hungry men coming in for lunch."

It was then Autumn realized that today Marsha was supposed to leave.

"Marsha, weren't you supposed to leave for Texas today?"

"I was, but how could I leave now? I sent a wire to a friend of mine in Texas, I explained what happened here and told her I may be a day or two late. She will take care of my mother and handle things till I get there."

Autumn went to the kitchen to start cooking, Marsha turned to see a man walking in the saloon.

"I'm sorry sir we're closed for now, there was a town tragedy."

"Yes I know, my cousins told me. I'm here to see my sister, Autumn."

"Oh you must be Ronnie. I'm sorry, she wasn't expecting you till closer to supper time."

"Yes I know, but I couldn't wait to get here so I left a little early. is she here?"

At that moment Autumn came out of the kitchen.

"Marsha do we have any..."

She saw Ronnie then ran to him and hugged him till he just about couldn't breathe.

"I thought you would be here later?"

"I couldn't wait, I left a little early. So what happened here?"

Autumn poured him some coffee and they sat for a quick talk. Marsha took over in the kitchen to give them some privacy.

"I can't get into everything right now but later I'm cooking supper for you Logan and Noah at his house. We'll sit and fill in all the details then. I'm so glad you're safe and here."

"Sounds good to me, I'm headed over there now, I need to get cleaned up. Then I'll go help out at the orphanage. We'll talk later."

Ronnie left and Autumn went back to the kitchen.

"You and your brother seem to be close?"

"We are, it wasn't always like that but we are now."

Marsha looked at her and finally decided to ask her the big question.

"Sweetie do you want to talk about what happened back home? It would do you some good."

Autumn shut down and went on talking, but not about what happened. Marsha didn't press her, when she was ready she would talk.

"Sally is a sweet little girl, do you know anything about her?"

At least she was talking even if it wasn't about what happened at home.

"Sally is special. A special case that is, she was three years old when her father left his wife. Never left them a penny just up and went. She never did know why. It was a few months later the papers had a story. Man found dead in the river. Turned out it was her husband. She never did learn the full story."

Autumn looked like she may cry.

"How awful!"

"Two months later Sally's mother caught tuberculosis and died, shortly later on, they found Sally next to her mother on the bed crying because she wouldn't wake up. No one had seen her mother around town so the sheriff went over to check on her and found Sally."

"Oh dear God that poor child!"

"We better get busy, it won't be long before we have a place full of hungry men."

Ronnie was with the other towns men helping to clean up so they could rebuild the orphanage. Trying to keep the town running with so many helping was not easy. So two men would run their business at a time in shifts.

They worked hard to clean up and get ready to build. Ronnie was filling a barrel when he heard a man scream. He turned in the direction and found a man pinned under a heavy wooden pillar. Quick as he could he rushed over to remove it but it was too heavy.

"Hey anybody, there's a man pinned over here, I need help."

Four men rushed over and removed the pillar as Ronnie pulled him out. He was having difficulty breathing. Logan rushed over to check him out.

"Let's get to my office fast."

He and Ronnie carried the man back to the office and Logan was in the room doing everything he could to try and save him. Ronnie waited outside to hear how the man was doing. When he turned, Logan was coming out of the room.

"He didn't make it, the pillar crushed his lungs."

That was something Ronnie did not want to hear. Without a word he hurried back to the site and in anger really moved the rubble out of there. Everyone took one look at Ronnie and knew the man died. He was tired of death, first his parents now this man, why? All this man did was try to help for the orphans, none of this made any sense. By that evening all the rubble would be gone and cleaned up ready to rebuild.

After lunch Marsha helped Autumn clean up so she could keep her promise to Sally, she knew they were both looking forward to seeing each other.

"Why don't you get ready to see Sally, I'll finish things here."

"Are you sure?"

"Go."

Hurrying as fast as she could to get ready and pick up Sally, Autumn was just as excited to see her as Sally would be to see Autumn. She came downstairs and rushed out the door. Marsha stood there with a smile on her face.

When Autumn walked over to the church she opened the door, there was Father Morgan with the children gathered around so he could tell them a story. Sally turned around and saw Autumn standing there. She ran to Autumn anxiously waiting to go out for the afternoon.

"I'll try not to keep her out very long."

Father Morgan didn't mind at all, Sally could use some time with someone instead of being alone.

"There's no problem, it will be good for her."

Sally waved goodbye to the other children and Father Morgan. They walked out of the church and started through town. Sally stopped at a window looking at a doll. She couldn't take her eyes off of it, it was just like the one she used to have.

"Do you like that doll?"

"Oh yes, she looks just like mine. I mean the one I use to have. When the sheriff came to get me when my mother wouldn't wake up, I didn't have time to take her. Amelia was my best friend, but now she's gone."

Autumn saw how sad she was.

"Let's go in and look around, OK?"

Sally looked at her with a big smile. They went into the store and while Sally was looking around Autumn bought the doll for her. Sally didn't seem much interested in anything else, so they left.

"Sally I bought you a present, open it, go ahead."

She was surprised to see the doll and so very excited.

"Oh boy, for me?" "Yes, for you." "Amelia, you're back."

25

Sally hugged the doll tight as if never to let her go again. They walked on down the street to the general store. Autumn wanted to pick up some sewing thread and needles. The store owner saw Sally and said hello.

"So how are you today?"

"I'm fine, Miss Autumn and me are spending the day together."

He giggled a bit.

"You mean Miss Autumn and I, not me."

"No, me and Miss Autumn."

They giggled and Autumn explained to her what the man meant by what he said, but she was so happy to have Amelia back she didn't even care. Autumn put her merchandise on the counter.

"May I also have a bagful of licorice? I want to take it to the church for the kids."

"Yes mam, one bag coming up, and no charge for the licorice." "Thank you so much."

The day was pretty hot out, the sun beating down. Autumn had an idea, she and Sally went to the dress shop and bought each of them swim suits. Sally looked up at her puzzled.

"How about we go swimming. I know of a lake near here where we can go. Would you like that?"

"Oh yes, that would be really fun. Only, what about Amelia?"

"Well she can watch us, you know keep an eye on us. Okay?"

"Sure! Do you hear that Amelia, you can watch us."

After shopping they went to the livery stable to use the wagon Ronnie brought. They put their packages in the wagon and rode to the lake. It was a covered wagon so they were able to change inside. Sally was looking around at the sites and enjoying herself.

"There are pretty places around here." Autumn was curious.

"Haven't you been around yet?"

"No Miss Autumn, living at the orphanage we don't leave town much. Not at all since I came to live here."

Even though it was understandable why they never left town it was also kind of sad. The children never had much to do, they need more fun in their lives. She knows the orphanage did their best. Finally they arrived at the lake. Sally's eyes were wide open.

"Oh boy, look how pretty it is here!"

"Okay, I'll change first while you and Amelia admire the site. Then you can change and Amelia can sit under the tree while we swim."

This was a real treat for Sally. Since she lost her mother and father there wasn't much for her or the other children to do, they could draw and play games but they weren't able to go outside of town. After Autumn changed she sent Sally in the wagon to change while she watched Amelia. Autumn hopped down from the wagon when Sally came out.

"Okay I'm ready."

They took a blanket from the wagon and spread it out underneath a tree nearby. Amelia was set down leaning against the tree then Autumn and Sally went to the lake. Autumn, Ronnie, Logan and Noah use to come here to swim when they were younger, the rope they use to swing from and drop in the water with was still there. Noah must have changed it at some point, it wasn't rotted out. She was sure he still came here to swim.

"Come here Sally, put your arms around my neck and hold on tight."

The water in that part of the lake wasn't that deep. Autumn grabbed onto the rope and put her foot in the loop, swung a few times then let go and splashed into the water. Autumn stood up and held on to Sally.

"Wow, that was a lot of fun. Can we do that again?"

It was good to see Sally smiling, it did Autumn some good also. For that time her troubles were left far behind, she was concentrating on Sally too much to think about her problems. For a while they splashed and swam, just enjoying their time together. After about an hour or so they dressed and headed back to town. She promised the boys she would cook them a special dinner.

Autumn walked Sally to the church and she couldn't wait to tell Father Morgan what fun they had together. Father saw them walk in and approached them

"So did you have a good time today?"

"Oh yes Father, I want to tell you what fun we had."

"Of course you can but for now you need to wash up and get ready for dinner. We can talk about you outing later."

"Yes Father. Good-bye Miss Autumn."

They waved good-bye then Autumn left heading back to the saloon. Marsha was there waiting to hear about their time together, but then the look on her face said it all.

"Marsha, those poor children don't really get to do much. That needs to change, they're kids and they need fun in their lives."

"You're right, but what can be done?"

Autumn thought for a moment, there must be something, then she had an idea.

"There's plenty, here's what I'm thinking."

They sat down and talked over her plans, Marsha thought it was a great idea and wished she could be there to help her.

"Marsha, could you come over to Noah's tonight for supper? I'm cooking more than enough and it would be nice to have another female around. Please?"

Marsha smiled and couldn't resist.

"Are you sure you want me there?"

"Of course I do, you're a part of our family."

Autumn had more in mind than just a special dinner for her and the boys, Marsha was leaving in the morning and she wanted to give her a proper send off. Autumn baked a cake at Noah's in the morning, she left it set till she could finish it for dinner. While she was shopping Autumn bought a beautiful gift for a going away present. She was going to Texas to face some hard times herself.

When Autumn walked through the door Noah was sitting at the table.

"Hello, I heard you had a fun day today?"

"I had a great day, by the way I invited Marsha for supper. I hope you boys don't mind? She's leaving in the morning for Texas and I wanted to make her last evening here special."

Noah shook his head, Autumn was always doing things for others. It was a good thing for her, keeping busy is just what she needs.

> "Heck no we don't mind, she's always been like a member of the family. Can't think of anyone who doesn't care about her."

Autumn went to work cooking and finishing the cake. She seemed happy keeping busy and doing for others, it was good for her. The aroma filled the house and the boys were ready for supper. She set the table making sure everything was in place. Noah was looking out the window and saw Marsha headed their way.

> "Here she comes."

Logan met her at the door welcoming her in, Ronnie was pleased to meet her again and Noah offered her a seat.

> "Autumn, everything smells so good, I hope you didn't put yourself out?"

> "No it's no trouble at all. I enjoy cooking for family."

Ronnie poured some wine for everyone, they were all called to table ready to eat. Logan spoke and offered to say grace.

> "Everything looks and smells delicious. May I say grace?"

> They bowed their heads for the blessing of the food and a safe trip for Marsha. "Okay everyone, let's eat."

They all enjoyed the meal, the company and conversation. When they finished Ronnie brought out the cake.

> "Marsha, everyone in this town and in this house loves you. We'll miss you, take with you our blessings. Maybe someday you can visit us. We'll be thinking about you and your mother."

> "Thank you Ronnie, thank you all. I love all of you as well."

Autumn gave her the present she bought for her. It was a beautiful silver music box. Marsha loved it, the exact one she was looking at through the window for a few weeks now. Little did she know Autumn saw her looking at it the day before.

"Thank you all again, each of you are in my heart, as much as I hate to go I really have to be going. I have to get up early. Autumn, I know you'll take care of my saloon as I would. Take care, things will get better."

Autumn went to hug her and wish her a safe trip.

"Please keep in touch when you can, I know you'll have your hands full but we would love to hear from you."

"Thank you and I will."

Ronnie walked Marsha back to the saloon while the others helped to clean up. Autumn poured a glass wine for her Noah and Logan then sat on the porch to enjoy the evening and unwind. There was a slight breeze and the moon so big and bright you could almost reach out and touch it, the light filled the town so peaceful and quiet.

"Well boys I had a big day, I think I'll go home and turn in for the night."

Noah smiled at her.

"Thanks for a great meal. You seem to be adjusting really well."

"I'm trying. The people here are very friendly and it does feel like everyone here is family. Well good night."

Noah offered to walk her home but she wanted to have some time to herself. She noticed signs were being put up, being curious she read one of them.

Big dance this Saturday to benefit the orphanage.

It's been a while since Autumn has even been to a dance and being new in town and not knowing anyone was no help. Maybe there was some other way she could contribute for the cause. She would talk to Father Morgan the next day and see how she could help, until then she was tuckered out and just wanted to go to bed. The day was a long one but a great one. Ronnie caught her looking at the sign.

"You love dances, are you thinking about going?"

She turned and looked at Ronnie.

"I don't think so, I don't know anyone and I wouldn't feel right attending myself. I want to see if there's a way I can contribute without attending."

Ronnie knew she loved dancing more than anything.

"Well, maybe Noah or Logan know of someone you can go with."

Autumn didn't care for that idea, being paired off with someone she didn't know was not appealing to her.

"No thanks, I wouldn't feel comfortable going with someone I don't know. Well I'm going to turn in for the night. Have a good night and I'll see you tomorrow."

She walked across the road to go home, a new home to get used to and a saloon to run. There are a lot of adjustments in store for her, she may not have time to have a social life. Once she gets her life put together she'll know better what she can and can't do.

Logan also decided to head home and turn in, he has a long schedule for the next day. Noah and Ronnie sat having some coffee and talking, catching up on things, talking about future plans. They all understood Autumn was struggling but it couldn't have been easy on Ronnie either.

"Ronnie, we know how Autumn is but what about you? She is clearly going through a difficult time but I can't tell how you are."

Ronnie has been so busy he hasn't had time to think much about it, or maybe that's his way of coping with things. If nothing else he was angry about things and how they turned out. Never once did he ever think anything like what happened would.

"I'm fine, I have to be. I'm the man of the family now."

Noah knew he was covering but he did need his time to grieve also.

"Look, what happened was nothing less than evil, it never should have happened but it did and you have a right to your feelings and to grieve."

Ronnie just stared out to the town, no emotions or even facial expressions.

"I'm more concerned with Autumn, I can't really tell how she's doing.

The night you and Logan left for Anaconda I went back in the house after checking on the horses and I heard her crying. I let her alone to have time for her but nothing has changed. I can't explain it but something has happened to her and until she breaks through that, I just don't know what to expect."

Noah knew he spoke the truth, but at the same time she couldn't be forced to let go of whatever it is that's happening with her. That could do more harm than good.

"I know what you mean, Logan and I notice it too." Ronnie was really concerned for her.

"I'm afraid she's headed for a breakdown."

"Look, we're all here for her and maybe it will take her a little longer. In any case she has all of us on her side. Whatever happens, we'll be there for her."

It was late and they were both exhausted. They turned in for the night, she had to let go at some point and like Noah said, she has all of them on her side. With each passing day she had to get better, and so would Ronnie.

The next morning Autumn was up early to sit with Marsha at the train station. In a short time they grew very close and Autumn hated to see her leave but knew she had no choice.

"Marsha I will miss you. I hope things go well back in Texas, but if there is anything, anything at all I can do, please let me know."

Marsha appreciated Autumn and her concern.

"The only thing you can do for me is take care of this place. It's been good to me and it will for you too, I'll write to you."

Autumn was happy that they would stay in touch.

"Take care, you have our blessings."

"You have my blessings."

Marsha knew Autumn was going through a difficult time, all she could do was pray for her and Ronnie to heal. Autumn stayed there and they waved good bye until the train was out of sight. It was a nice morning, not too hot and a cool breeze, the sun was shining. Strolling back to the saloon slowly and just enjoying the morning was relaxing to Autumn. She was so lost in the morning nothing around her phased her. Until a man yelled out to her.

"Look out."

He ran to her and pulled her out of the pathway of a fast moving stagecoach. At that moment she realized what may have happened and was shaken a little.

"Oh my...thank you so much. I reckon I wasn't paying attention."

He smiled at her.

"No I reckon not, but you're fine now. By the way I'm Austin McAvoy, I'm new in town. It's nice to meet you."

Autumn noticed how handsome he is, she was a little flustered.

"Hello I'm Autumn Snyder, I just moved here, my cousins live here, it's nice to meet you. Thank you so much again."

All she could think was too much information.

"Well I'm pleased to meet you miss. I am kind of hungry, would you happen to know a good place around here to grab some grub?"

"Well you see that saloon over there, Pearl Star?" "Yes."

She never mentioned she was the one who owns the place.

"My cousins say they have pretty good food."

Austin tipped his hat and smiled.

"Much obliged Miss. Hope to see you around again."

Autumn couldn't help but smile as he walked to the saloon.

"Sooner than you think."

She said to herself and walked over and went in the back way to the kitchen. After she put on her apron she went out to the table where Austin was sitting to take his order.

"May I help you?"

He was surprised to see her again and so soon.

"Well hello again. So you work here?"

"No, I actually own this place. So what can I get for you?"

He smiled thinking he will like living here after all.

"I'd like a stack of hot cakes and some bacon, coffee if it's not too much trouble."

"Be right back."

She turned and went back to the kitchen, then returned with a cup of coffee.

"Enjoy your coffee, breakfast will be out shortly."

So far he seemed to like it in this town, things were getting off to a good start. While he waited he pulled out some papers to look over, he was in town for a job a friend of his had told him about. As he began looking over a letter he received from his friend when his friend walked in and sat down.

"Noah, how are you?"

"I'm good, glad you made it here."

Noah noticed he had a big smile on his face.

"So what's the big smile for?"

"I met someone today. Well we don't know each other but I saved her from being run down by a stagecoach. She's a beauty."

"Oh yeah, so when can I meet her?"

Autumn was bringing out his breakfast when she saw Noah.

"Here you are, Noah what brings you here?"

Austin was stunned, wondering how Noah knew this woman.

"You two know each other?"

Autumn was smiling.

"Autumn is my cousin. She and her brother just moved here a couple of days ago."

Austin didn't know what to say.

"Enjoy your grub. Noah would you like anything?"

"If it's not trouble what he's having looks good. Thanks."

Austin was eating so he wouldn't have to talk.

"So you seem to like my cousin."

He swallowed his food then sipped some coffee.

"Sorry Noah, if you prefer I didn't..."

"No it's okay, I think you may be able to help her."

She didn't look like she needed any help, so he didn't understand.

"She and her brother moved here because their parents were brutally murdered. It's been really hard on her and we're all worried about her. We don't mind, just take it easy on her that's all."

Suddenly Austin felt bad for her.

"Maybe I should pass."

Noah didn't mean to change his mind, he just wanted him to go easy on her.

"No, forget what I told you. Look there's a dance this Saturday, ask her to go with you."

"I don't know, do you think she will?"

"She loves dances, what will it hurt to ask?"

They talked more about the job Austin was in town for. Autumn brought out breakfast for Noah then left the men to talk. Back in the kitchen she was preparing lunch for the men who had been working on the new building for the orphanage. Noah came back to the kitchen to say goodbye.

"Austin left some money on the table for his breakfast, so did I. He has business to tend to and I have to go to the orphanage site. Things keep going like they are those kids will have a new home in no time."

"That sounds wonderful. Lunch will be ready for everyone, I'm making chili."

Noah hugged her and promised he would let everyone know about lunch.

"Hey, how is Logan? Will he be stopping over?"

"Not today but if you want I'd be happy to take him some. I'm sure he would love some chili."

Autumn smiled and told him it would be ready. While the chili was simmering she went to set the tables and have everything ready. She picked up the money Austin left her then noticed a slip of paper with something written on it so she started to read his message. He wanted to have dinner with her that night, and he would get back to her in a couple of hours. She was flattered and had time to think about it, she wasn't sure she should. Logan walked in to see how she was doing.

"Hello sweetie, how is everything ?"

"Everything is going very well thank you. Marsha is on her way to Texas and I have chili simmering for lunch. Noah was just here, he didn't think you would be stopping in today!"

"Well I have a quick moment and I wanted to check up on you. Chili, is it your father's recipe? He made great chili."

"Yes it is, none other, and I'm fine thank you though for your concern." Logan couldn't wait for lunch."

"Oh would you happen to know Austin McAvoy also?"

"Yes I do, Noah told him about a job here in town. Austin has been wanting to move here for a long time now. His father was abusive and his mother had a nervous breakdown. She's in a home not far from here so he's been wanting to move here to be near her."

"What ever happened to his father?"

Logan shook his head, it was terrible things turned out like this. Especially for Austin's mother.

"He doesn't know, he left and no one has ever heard from him. I hate to leave but I really have to get back. Count me in for lunch. See you later."

She went back to setting the tables for lunch then went to check on her chili. The aroma was delectable, brought back memories of her father. There was a knock at her back door. Victoria, the school teacher was standing there with boxes.

"Hello, my name is Victoria. I teach school here in town. I heard you were fixing lunch for the men working on the orphanage and I wanted to offer these pies I baked. That's if you don't mind."

Autumn was getting to know everyone a little at a time, it was unfortunate it was due to the orphanage burning down.

"Please come in, that would be perfect. My name is..."

"You don't have to tell me, you're Autumn Snyder. Cousin of Logan and Noah. People around town have heard about you and your brother. Logan talks about you as well as Noah. In a good way of course. I am sorry to hear about your parents.

"Thank you. Would you like some coffee?" Victoria set the pies on the table.

"I would love some thank you. Whatever you're cooking sure smells delicious."

"You're welcome to try some."

They were getting along very well. It would be nice to have a friend in town, especially since Marsha had to leave and Victoria seemed very friendly.

"I don't want to put you to any trouble."

"No trouble at all. Please sit down."

They sat and talked over coffee, getting to know each other. Victoria was engaged to a man in town, Tim Birescik. They met through a catalog she listed herself in and he found her to be interesting. A few months back he wrote to her and they arranged to meet. They courted since then and now they are to be hitched.

"Maybe that all sounds unconventional, but the men I use to meet were not appealing. When I met Tim he was different, caring. Not like the

ones I was use to, they just seemed egotistical. Not Abe, he makes me
feel like a lady, like I'm special."

"As long as you're happy nothing else matters, not even how you met.
As long as you're in love."

Victoria was so glad to hear her say that, many women believed what she did was wrong
but they are so in love. They enjoyed each others company so much the time just flew away.

"Well the men will be coming in for lunch, I really enjoyed our talk."

Victoria smiled, Autumn was the first woman in town who didn't judge her.

"So did I, could you use some help? I'd love to stay and work with you
if you don't mind?"

"That would be great thank you so much."

The two women started filling trays with bowls of chili and the pie Victoria made to serve
the hungry men. When they came in Autumn would take out the trays to serve while Victoria
filled the trays. Things were easier with another woman to help. After lunch was served to
everyone Autumn served Victoria.

"Here you are, sit and eat. It's the least I can do for your help."

"Thank you so much, and I did save two pieces of pie for us."

The men went on about how much they enjoyed the chili and the pie. Autumn and Victoria
sat down to eat and Victoria really seemed to enjoy it herself.

"Autumn I've eaten chili before but never as tasty as this."

"Well thank you, it's my father's recipe. He cooked it on camping trips
he would take us on, we had great times together."

Victoria saw her eyes light up when she talked about her father.

"Did your mother go with you?"

"No she didn't, she never cared for camping. We had our times together
too, she taught me how to cook and bake, everything. I could talk to
her about anything. Our family was very close." Victoria saw her eyes
growing sad, she didn't mean to upset her.

"I'm sorry, I shouldn't have brought this up."

"No, it's okay really. I seemed to have blocked out what happened. I can't remember, but I thank God I can remember the good times. They will always be mine."

Victoria smiled offering to be there for her anytime. There was a knock at the door and Autumn answered.

"Yes, how may I help you?"

There stood a man she doesn't recall ever seeing.

"Yes mam, are you Autumn Snyder?" "Who wants to know?"

"Well I was helping out with the orphanage site and there was was an accident. I'm sorry to say but your brother was hurt. You better come right away."

Autumn wasn't sure she should go, it was strange. If this were true why didn't one of her cousins come to tell her.

"I don't recall seeing you around here."

"I'm from the next town over, when I heard about the orphanage I come to help."

"I don't understand, why didn't my cousin come to tell me?"

"They are trying to help him. I don't mean to rush you but you really need to come."

She was confused but didn't want to take any chances.

"Autumn you go on, I'll stay here till you get back."

Autumn picked up her wrap and left the man.

"I don't even know your name but you know mine."

After she hopped up on the wagon he pulled out a gun.

"My name doesn't matter, just keep quiet and you won't get hurt."

Her stomach felt nauseous and she was frightened, not knowing what this was all about.

"Why are you doing this? What is this about?"

"You'll find out soon enough just sit and don't let on anything is wrong, if you do you're dead."

All she could do was remain quiet and scared. What did he want? Just a few minutes later Logan went to the saloon for lunch.

"Autumn I'm ready for some of that delicious chili."

Victoria came out with a tray of chili and pie.

"Hey, is Autumn here?"

"No she isn't. I'm Victoria, I told her I would stay here until she came back."

Logan was curious.

"Back from where?"

"The orphanage site, a man came to the door and said her brother was hurt badly and she should go with him."

"Are you sure? I just came from there and Ronnie is fine. There were no accidents."

"Oh no, where did he take her?"

Victoria had fear on her face and Logan had no idea what was happening.

"You better come with me, you shouldn't stay here by yourself."

Together they went to the site to let Ronnie and Noah know what happened. Noah looked at Victoria.

"Do you know what this man looked like?"

"Yes, I do. He had on a black hat, green plaid shirt and brown pants and chaps and he wore a dark brown brick hat. Oh and he said he's from the next town over, that was all he said as far as that. Please help her!"

Noah looked at her face and saw her concern for Autumn.

>"We will find him, both of them you can count on that." Ronnie's face had anger on him.

>"What is going on, why would anyone want to take Autumn?"

Logan and Noah tried to calm him down assuring him they would find her.

>"If he harms one hair on her head..."

>"Ronnie, calm down. You know we will find her. Now is there anyone that you know of who would want to hurt her for any reason?"

Ronnie was quiet, for sure it couldn't be the man who attacked the Indian woman, her brother killed him.

>"I can't think of anyone who would want to harm her, then again that was the same issue with our parents."

Noah and Ronnie set out to search for her, Logan stayed behind in case someone tried to contact the family. Victoria was headed back to the saloon.

>"Wait, where are you going?"

>"I'm going to take care of things at the saloon for her."

>"No you shouldn't be there alone, I'll go with you and we'll close it down till she comes back."

Logan and Victoria walked together and hung a sign on the door, closed until further notice. While they were inside Victoria went to the kitchen to put things away. On the table was a note. She picked it up to read it then ran to show it to Logan.

>"Look, I found this on the table, it wasn't here when we left!"

He read the note then went searching for his brother. He had taken Victoria with him to stay with the others on site until he returned, then he went to Noah's house. When he arrived Noah and Ronnie were getting ready to leave.

>"I'm glad I caught up with you. Victoria found this on the table in the kitchen at the saloon. We went over to lock up and put up a closed sign. Any ideas?"

Jeanette Kossuth McAdoo

Noah read the note.

YOU KILLED MY BROTHER, IF YOU WANT YOUR COUSIN BACK SAFELY, MEET ME AT THE COPPER MINE. IF NOT, YOU WILL NEVER SEE HER AGAIN.

He had no idea who it was, there were so many he killed just in defense. It could be anyone.

> "I'm going right now."

> "You're not going alone I'm going with you. She is my sister."

> "No, you stay here, this is between me and which ever person who holds a grudge against me. I'll bring her back safely. I can promise you that."

Ronnie didn't like it but Noah knew what he was doing. He is the best. Ronnie and Logan went inside the house to wait. The most difficult thing to do.

> "I know this may not be of any help but I go through this every time he goes out on a bounty, and I know this is your sister involved but just because we're cousins doesn't mean we don't feel the same or worry the same way you are right now. You have to believe when Noah says he'll bring her back safely, he will."

Ronnie poured them both a glass of whiskey and nodded his head.

> "This is what you go through every time he goes out?"

> "I use to, a lot when he decided to hunt bounty's, but now I'm use to it and the only reason I am is because he is the best. He's proved that time and time again."

Deep down Ronnie knew it too, but now this is his sister. He wasn't as use to this as Logan is, but he had to be strong once again. They sat quietly, no words spoken. Just worrying, the tension was unbearable. Ronnie looked up and saw Austin walking up to the porch.

> "I just heard about Autumn, is there anything I can do to help?"

Ronnie sat there while Logan expressed his appreciation for his offer.

> "Right now there's nothing but thank you. My brother is handling everything. He will bring her back."

Austin took one look at Ronnie and knew it would be best if he didn't say anything to him, that was understandable. He turned and walked away.

The men were still working on the site, Victoria walked around town praying for Autumn and hoping Noah would bring her home soon. Father Morgan had heard about Autumn's kidnapping and stopped by the house to see Ronnie.

> "I just heard about your sister. I'm sorry, Sally keeps asking about her. I just told her she went away for a short time and will be back. Sally loves her, we all do."

Ronnie looked up at Father Morgan.

> "Thank you Father. We have hope she will be back soon. Please excuse me."

Logan and Father Morgan watched as he stood up and went inside the house.

> "I'm sorry Father, he's been through so much and now with Autumn."

> "It's ok I understand. I'll be praying for all of you. Have a blessed day."

Then he turned and walked away.

> "Doctor Logan, I fell and scraped my knee pretty bad. Could you please help me?"

> "Of course, come on up on the porch. I'll get my bag."

The little boy is the son of the towns blacksmith.

> "So how did this happen Jimmy?"

He looked at Logan and smiled.

> "Zack and I were racing, only I fell an hit my knee hard."

> "Well you be careful you don't want to break anything, like your bones. If you do that it will take a long time to heal and you won't be able to play for a while. OK?"

> "Yes sir, thank you doctor Logan."

> "There you are, good as new. Now slow down a bit."

Meanwhile Noah was on his way to the mine to find Autumn and bring her back. When he arrived at the entrance there was a note on the ground sticking out from under a rock. He picked up the note and all it said was::

KNOW WHO I AM?

All this did was anger him more. Slowly and carefully he entered the mine. He lit a candle and started walking till he could find who was behind this. Noah heard a noise, like a rock falling.

"Stay where you are."

Noah heard the man but still couldn't see him. The man stepped out from behind a rock.

"Now do you know who I am?"

Noah recognized him and nodded his head.

"What do you want Amos? Why bring Autumn in on this?"

"You know why, you killed my brother."

"Wrong, you know what happened, it was an accident." Amos squinted his eyes.

"It was an accident that should not have happened if it hadn't been for you."

Noah looked around and didn't see his cousin anywhere.

"Where is she?"

"Awww you worried about her?"

"I said where is she?"

Amos laughed an evil laugh then pointed behind him.

"There's your precious cousin. Surrender to me and I'll let her go."

Autumn was tied up on the ground screaming through the scarf tied around her mouth and shaking her head no. Amos had a gun pointed right at her. "So what's it going to be?"

"Let her go and I'll surrender, hurt her before and you're a dead man."

He kept a gun on Noah until he untied her, once she was he let her go and she ran to Noah in tears.

> "It's okay, your fine. My horse is out there, take him and get out of here."

> "I can't leave you behind."

> "You have to now."

Autumn did as he told her, reluctantly. Then Amos went on talking about his victory and how he would watch Noah die as his brother did. Noah had a key chain he made. Once he killed a rattle snake and kept the rattle.

> "Look out a snake!"

Noah cried out.

> "Forget it you're not fooling me."

Noah shook the key chain and Amos looked down to shoot it, when he did the noise caused the mine to collapse, Noah got out as quickly as he could. Autumn heard the cave falling in and panicked until she saw Noah running out and the entrance, the cave collapsing as he made it out. Noah rushed over to her, she was in tears.

> "It's fine, it's over. Let's go home."

Noah helped her on his horse then he hopped up and they left for home.

Chapter 3

Logan went back to the house to check on Ronnie, he was sitting on the porch drinking whiskey.

> "All the whiskey in the world won't change things, he will bring her back."

Just then some towns people were cheering, when Logan and Ronnie looked up they saw Autumn and Noah riding towards the house. Ronnie went running to meet them, pulled Autumn off the horse and held her tight. Everyone was so happy she was back and safe. Victoria and Sally saw her, they came running over to hug her.

"I'm fine really, thank you all so much."

Ronnie looked at Noah.

"Where is he, I want him."

"I'm sorry but you can't have him. I just made it out of the cave when it collapsed, he's dead."

Ronnie said no more, he was thankful Autumn was back and safe. Logan walked over to welcome her home safe and unharmed.

"Would you mind if I got in on the hugging?"

Sally and Victoria were so happy to see her again. Autumn looked at all of them.

"It's so great to be home. So how about I cook dinner and we all celebrate my coming back home. Victoria will you help me?"

"Absolutely."

Sally looked up feeling left out.

"Well don't just stand there we can use you too."

Sally and Autumn laughed and the three of them went inside. Sally had Amelia with her.

"Miss Autumn, Amelia missed you too. We were both crying, we didn't think we would ever see you again."

Autumn felt bad she went through the worry, Sally has been through enough in her life.

"Sally, I will never leave you and Amelia. I will always be here for both of you. Okay?"

Tears came to Sally's eyes as she nodded her head and reached for a hug.

When Autumn stood up she saw Austin in the doorway standing there staring at her.

"Welcome home, it's good to see you back and safe."

"Thank you. You asked me out for supper tonight, how about you stay for supper here?"

He smiled, he was glad to see she is safe and back home.

> "Well I did have something a little more quiet in mind but, I'd be honored to stay. Thank you."

The men all sat outside while the women cooked supper.

> "Autumn, I still have two pies left over. Why don't I run over to the saloon and bring them here for later?"

> "That sounds great thank you."

She didn't want Victoria walking by herself, not after today so she asked Ronnie to walk her over and back. Austin pulled out a harmonica from his pocket and played. They could hear him playing inside, they all enjoyed themselves so much and they were all together. Tonight there were no troubles for anyone.

> "Miss Autumn, that man is playing music."

> "Yes he is isn't he."

Sally started dancing around with Amelia enjoying the music. So much that Victoria and Autumn joined in, this evening had turned into a party. Ronnie and Victoria walked in with Father Morgan.

> "Autumn, Father Morgan is here for Sally."

Sally stopped dancing and wasn't ready to leave yet, she wanted to stay and have fun with Autumn.

> "Miss Snyder, I'm very sorry but it's time for Sally to come back."

She was so disappointed, she was enjoying herself and felt like she was part of a family again. Autumn pulled Father Morgan aside and asked if she could spend the night if she promised to have her back the next morning after breakfast. One look at Sally's face and he couldn't refuse.

> "Sally, you can spend the night with Miss Snyder but you have to be back tomorrow right after breakfast."

Sally was so excited she went over to Father Morgan and gave him a great big hug.

> "Thank you so much, I'll be a good girl. Promise."

"I'm sure you will. Take care and I'll see you tomorrow."

Autumn asked Father Morgan if he would like to stay for supper, but he could not. He had the other children to take care of but he thanked her then was on his way. After he left she and Victoria served supper. This evening was more like a party than just supper, everyone was enjoying themselves. Laughing, dancing and even singing.

A few hours later Sally had fallen asleep, Autumn thought now is the time to take her home and put her to bed.

"Good night everyone, this has been a joyful evening."

Everyone said goodnight and thanked the ladies for a great meal. Austin carried Sally to Autumn's room and they tucked her in for the night.

"Thank you so much for carrying her all the way over here."

"No trouble, she's a cute little girl. Thank you for supper, it was delicious."

"Why thank you, it was nice of you to stay. I wanted to make it up to you. I know it wasn't the evening you had in mind..."

"No it wasn't, but it was still a great time. You're lucky you have a terrific little family. They care a great deal about you."

Autumn stopped to think, she was lucky. She does have family but Austin doesn't. "Autumn, may I ask you a question."

"Okay."

"I was hoping you would honor me at the dance this Saturday?"

Smiling and playing a little coy, she did accept.

"I would love to go with you. Thank you, right now though I'm really exhausted. Would you mind terribly?"

"Not at all, that was a load of excitement in one day. Sleep well."

"Thank you, and thank again you for helping me with Sally. Good night."

Austin tipped his hat before he left, then hugged Autumn and went on his way. After he left she walked over and stared at Sally for a few minutes. All she could think about is what a sweet child Sally is, she deserved a family, all those children did. Autumn wanted to do more for those children than just attend a dance but what? They not only lost their home but their beds, clothes blankets and their personal things. Children shouldn't have to go through this tragedy. She crawled in bed with Sally then went to sleep.

The next morning Autumn had breakfast ready for Sally so she could take her back to Father Morgan as she promised.

"How is your breakfast?"

Sally had her mouth full and did her best to smile and nodded her head. Autumn giggled a bit knowing she meant she loved breakfast. Victoria came in to help Autumn.

"Good morning."

"Good morning. What brings you here so early?"

"Well I thought you could use some help, if that's okay?"

Autumn smiled at her with a bit of relief on her face.

"That would be wonderful, thank you so much. So if I'm not prying, when do we get to meet your fiance?"

Victoria knew that question would come up and was waiting.

"Well we really didn't get to talk yesterday but he'll be back in town today. We've been planning on getting hitched but he had some family business to tend to out of town."

Autumn had a concerned look on her face.

"Nothing serious I hope."

"No nothing like that. His mother lives in Rexburg Idaho and she had sold her farm. His mother is getting older and it became difficult for her to run the farm. She doesn't want to move here, she loves Idaho so he helped her to sell the farm and move to a smaller place." "Will she be all right on her own?"

"Oh yes, she's feisty but the farm was too much. Before she lost her husband they ran the farm for many years. Tim was born and raised there. She just wanted a more simple life now."

The two woman drank coffee and talked to each other, they were becoming close. Sally finished her breakfast and was ready to leave, not that she wanted to but she and Autumn did promise Father Morgan she would be back after breakfast.

"Victoria would you mind taking care of things here for a few minutes? I have to take Sally back to the church."

"I'd be happy to, take care Sally. Hope we'll see you again."

"Me too, I really like Miss Autumn. We always have fun together. Maybe someday you could come with us?"

The two woman laughed and looked at each other.

"I would like that Sally, thank you."

Victoria waved to Sally as they left then went to work in the kitchen making breakfast for the men. Autumn and Sally walked by the orphanage site and Sally just stared for a moment.

"Sally we should go."

"Do you reckon us kids will have a home again?"

It was all Autumn could do to keep from crying.

"Of course you will sweetie. Those men are going to rebuild it for all of you. It will be brand new, you'll see."

Sally smiled as they continued to go to the church. Father Morgan met them at the door. Sally clung on to Autumn saying good bye and hoping she would see her again. Autumn walked over to the site to see how things were progressing, slowly but surly.

"Autumn, how did things go last night with Sally?"

Ronnie was curious and believed Autumn is becoming attached to Sally as much as Sally is attached to Autumn.

"Everything went well, last night was great, it felt like we had a real family again. Will you and the men stop by for breakfast?"

Ronnie waved and told her they would be over shortly. Autumn walked in the saloon and found Victoria had breakfast ready.

"Victoria can you handle things down here for a bit, I need to take care of something?"

"Yes of course. Are you all right?"

"Yes I'm fine thank you."

She went to her room and gazed out the window, tears came to her eyes as she walked over to the bed to lay down and cry. Things were getting to her, she didn't understand why she couldn't remember what happened the night her parents were murdered. It were as though she lost part of her memory. Autumn looked at the picture of them at Christmas time.

"I can't remember and I don't know why this happened. What's wrong with me?"

She cried a little longer before pulling herself together and heading back downstairs. Maybe someday she'll get back her memory about what exactly happened. The men were all enjoying their breakfast and were heading back to the site. She gathered the dishes to take them to the kitchen to be washed. Autumn was about to go into the kitchen when a man walked through the door.

"May I help you?"

"I hope so, I'm Tim Birescik and I'm looking for Victoria."

"Oh yes, I'll send her out. It's really nice to meet you, I'm Autumn."

Autumn let Victoria know that Tim was waiting for her. She went to see him, stood there for a moment to get a look at him.

"Well don't just stand there, I've missed you."

She smiled an ran over to hug him, they couldn't seem to let go of each other.

"I have something for you,let me see your hand."

He took her left hand and slipped on a diamond ring his mother gave to him to pass on. Victoria gazed at it and couldn't believe it was on her finger.

"Tim it's beautiful, but how could you afford it, it must have cost hundreds of dollars?"

He smiled at her knowing how happy she is with the ring.

"No I didn't buy it, it was my mother's. When I told her about you and that we are getting hitched she gave me her ring. She insisted there was no way I could refuse. Do you really like the ring?"

"Yes I do, I'll have to write to her and thank her."

They were so happy together, all they needed now was a date.

"I know we can't have a regular wedding but I thought the town's justice of peace would hitch us."

Autumn couldn't help but over hear so she came in to talk to them both.

"Nonsense, we can hold a beautiful wedding right here. I'll take care of everything, my present to both of you."

Tim and Victoria looked at each other then Tim spoke.

"That is a very nice offer but we can't accept that, it's too much."

"Not really, I want to and I promise it will be beautiful. Please?"

Victoria had a look in her eyes and Tim knew she wanted this as much as Autumn wanted to do this for them. Finally Tim agreed and Autumn would start making plans that evening. Autumn told Victoria they would both go shopping after lunch, they both needed dresses, Victoria for her wedding and Autumn for the dance Saturday night.

"You know when Sally and I went shopping we stopped at the dress shop just to look around. They have a beautiful white dress that would be perfect for your wedding. You decide though, it is your wedding."

They arrived at the dress shop and Autumn pointed out the dress she was telling Victoria about. Autumn was right, the dress was beautiful.

"It is perfect, it looks very much like the dress my grandmother wore at her wedding. We don't know what ever happened to that dress. This is the one I will wear."

Victoria's eyes gleamed and she couldn't take her eyes off the dress. They found shoes and a veil, everything she needed. What a beautiful bride Victoria would be. After they found a dress for the wedding the searched for one for Autumn to wear at the dance Saturday.

There was a beautiful satin dress in the corner, two different shades of purple and shoes that matched the dress perfectly.

"Autumn look at this, it's breathtaking I think this is the one for you. It's so rich looking, this will look wonderful on you."

Purple is her favorite color and the dress does look fabulous. The two women tried on their dresses, both women looked divine. They paid for their merchandise then took them back to the saloon and put them away. The day seemed to be flying by, the men would be coming in for lunch soon. They came back downstairs to prepare when they found a man sitting at a table.

"Hello, may we help you?"

All he did was sit there staring at them, he never said a word. Again they asked if there was anything they could do for him. He pulled out a gun aiming right at them. Autumn pulled Victoria behind her.

"Don't come in here trying to scare us, we asked you a question? What do you want?"

No one saw Sally standing in the entrance, when she saw the man pull out his gun she ran for help. She was headed for the site where the men were working when suddenly she ran right into Noah.

"Whoa Sally slow down, what's your hurry?"

"Mr Noah, come quick. Miss Autumn and Miss Victoria need help!"
"Okay honey slow down and breath. Why do they need help?"

Sally took a deep breath then began to explain.

"There's a strange man at the saloon and he has a gun. He's aiming it at them. Please hurry!"

"Sally, are you sure that's what you saw?"

"Yes sir, please help them."

Noah called to Ronnie and they walked Sally over to Logan's office to keep her safe. Then Ronnie and Noah went to the saloon. Noah went in the front and Ronnie went in the back. When Noah quietly walked in he saw the man was Jake Adams, a bank robber he's been trying to track for a month now. Jake was not an easy one, every bounty hunter Noah knows has been looking for him.

"Jake drop your gun, now."

"Well well if it isn't Noah Evagues. How did you find me?"

"You're in my town and I don't take to outlaws dirtying my town, I'm here to clean up." Jake laughed taunting him.

"You really think you can take me?" Ronnie came in from behind. "Would you like to take a chance? You heard him, drop it now."

The women went behind the bar, nervous about what was going to happen.

"You may be slick but I promise you won't get out of this one."

Jake backed up just a bit towards the bar, the women saw him drop his gun but he had a knife sticking out of the back of his trousers. He reached for the knife when Autumn grabbed the gun behind the bar and shot him. Noah and Ronnie looked at her then checked on Jake, he was dead. Noah went to Autumn.

"It's okay honey, let go of the gun. It's over." Ronnie walked over, Autumn came around slowly.

"He had a knife he was going to pull it out and..."

Noah knew of his tricks.

"Don't worry you did fine. He was a dangerous man, you did the town a favor. This was bound to happen."

Autumn looked at them both.

"How did you know?"

Ronnie hugged her.

"Sally was here and saw him pull a gun on you. She ran to us for help. She's safe in Logan's office. She saved you two."

Autumn couldn't believe Sally saw what happened.

"Victoria would take care of things here please, I have to go see Sally."

"Of course."

Autumn rushed out the door and over to Logan's office. Bursting through the door she saw Sally sitting there crying and Logan tending to her. Autumn rushed over to her picking her up and hugging her.

"Sally it's fine. We're all fine thanks to you, you saved us."

Sally looked at her in disbelief.

"I did! Really? Did you hear that Amelia, we saved them."

Sally hugged her doll then Autumn, she was so happy to see her.

"You know what? Because you were so brave I'm making a special dinner just for you, Sunday at Mr Noah's house. Okay?"

"Oh boy, just for me?"

She was so excited, it's been a very long time since anyone made a special dinner for her for any reason.

"Can Amelia come too?"

"Well sure, it wouldn't be special without her."

After they made plans Autumn walked Sally back to the church and told her she would pick her up tomorrow for dinner. She hugged Sally and waited for her to go inside before she went back to the saloon. Autumn passed Ronnie and Noah as they were going back to the site.

"Autumn, we took care of everything. Victoria is fixing lunch so we'll see you then. Are you sure you're all right?"

"I am thank you both very much. See you soon."

Autumn and Victoria were talking about the orphanage being rebuilt.

"Victoria I've been thinking, after the orphanage is rebuilt it doesn't end there, they still need beds, blankets, clothes and food. The men can rebuild a building but what about the necessities?"

Autumn was right, those children needed more than just a building.

"Autumn, what if there was a way to raise money to buy those things?"
"What are you thinking about?"

"Well...we could ask for donations and hold a silent auction. We could even have a fair, music, pony rides, sell baked pies and cakes and such. Play some games, we can charge a fee for the games and pony rides. We can raise money that way."

Autumn thought for a moment and the more she thought about it the more she likes the idea.

"Victoria that is a dandy idea, I do believe it will work. We can talk to the other women in town and maybe they will help with baked and canned foods. Something!"

They heard the men talking in the next room waiting for lunch.

"Let's get them their lunch so we can put this in the works." Logan walked in after most of the men were served their lunch.

"Autumn, how are things going over here?"

"Hey Logan, I need to talk to you, do you have a minute?" "Anything for you sweetie, what's kick-en?"

Autumn seemed excited about something, it was good to see her this way. "Victoria I need to talk to my cousin, can you handle this?"

Victoria nodded and went about the daily work. Autumn and Logan sat at a table away from the others. She told him about the idea they had to raise money for the orphanage and asked for his help. Logan had many things he could donate for the auction and would even donate some money to help.

"What you need are some posters to hang, it would be easier letting people know what you're doing so they can help anyway they can. I know this town, they will help."

Autumn thought it was a wonderful idea. Logan knew the man who ran the paper and he could talk to him about printing up posters for her. Autumn wrote down as quickly as she could some information and who to talk to about the donations.

"This looks good, I'll run it over to Clay at the paper. I'm sure he'll have the posters in no time."

Autumn was excited, then she saw a look on Logan's face.

"Is something wrong?"

"I just want to be sure, are you really up to doing all this? You've been through so much, can you handle this too?"

Autumn understood what he meant.

"I sure am, this is helping me too. All I can think about are those children."

"Your chili would make some money, it's the best I ever ate."

Logan ate his lunch then went to the newspaper office. Autumn told Victoria how Logan would help. Hopefully this would be a success.

"Autumn, I know where we can get two ponies for the rides. Tim has a friend here in town and he has about three or four ponies."

"Wonderful, now I can spread the word to the women in town and see where we can go from there."

Everyone in town wanted to help one way or another. When one of the women in town heard about the fair, she offered to make a quilt to sell. There was two she had made for gifts next year but they could be redone. Another woman in town canned jams, she was going to work on that right away. Once word got out people offered what ever they could to raise money for the new orphanage.

Autumn had to go to the general store for some things for the saloon. When she walked in Mr. Holt met her with a box.

"Hey Miss Snyder, I heard about the fair you're planning to raise money for the orphanage, You are a very special and caring lady. Anyway I filled this box with things you could use as prizes for the games. If you need any thing else please let me know. Now I know you didn't come for the box so how can I help you?"

"Well thank you for the donation it will help. I have a small list of things I need for the saloon."

"Well you just leave that list with me and I'll bring everything over to you free of charge. It's the least I can do."

Autumn's day was getting off to a good start, so many people offering things to help raise money. Logan was right, people in town sure are willing to help. Autumn walked by the site where the men were working. What was left from the burned down building was cleaned up and the men were getting ready to start the new building. The day was perfect, not too hot. Ronnie saw Autumn and walked over to talk to her.

"Hey sis, how is everything going? I hear you're going to plan a fair to raise money for the orphanage? That's great, they will need it to get back their lives."

"They will, I've been thinking about this and I'm hoping we can raise enough to replace everything."

One of the men called for Ronnie, they needed his help.

"Well I have to get back, good luck."

The men were working hard and as quickly as they could to get those kids back again. The orphanage that burned down was a smaller building, the kids only had their rooms and the dining room. Ronnie had the idea to add one more room than before so they would have a place to play even in the bad weather. This would be a better building than before. He called the men together to plan for the extra room, it was agreed to build for the kids. They needed more than just a place to sleep and eat, they are kids.

It was Saturday morning and the dance was that evening. Austin stopped by the saloon to see Autumn. He walked in and she saw him when she came out from the kitchen.

"Hey Austin, what brings you here?"

"I just wanted to know if we're still going together to the dance, hope you didn't change your mind."

Autumn smiled at him, she was in a good mood nothing would spoil her time out this evening.

"No I haven't changed my mind, I'll be ready. What time should I expect you."

"Well I thought we could have supper at the hotel about six then go to the dance from there, if that works for you?"

"That sounds perfect, I'll see you at six."

Autumn went to her room to lay out her dress and everything she needed to get ready for the dance. She sat on the edge of her bed with the family picture in her hand talking to her mother and wishing she could be here with her.

"Mom, I really wish you were here, you always could fix my hair just right. I'm on my own now. Austin seems like a very nice man, I think you and dad would like him. I have a lot to keep me busy. I hope you and dad don't mind Ronnie and I sold the house, I just couldn't live there, not like that. I'm sorry. We love you both and miss you so much."

She put the picture back down on the stand then went to the window to look out. Autumn was feeling something, she couldn't figure it out. It's so frustrating that she can't remember, maybe she's not supposed to remember. Her thoughts were interrupted by Victoria calling to her.

"Autumn, could you please come back downstairs?"

"I'm coming."

Autumn went downstairs to find a group of women waiting for her.

"These women would like to talk with you."

Autumn thanked her then went over to speak with them.

"Good afternoon ladies, how may I help you?"

Word was out about the fair she was planning to raise money for the orphanage, all these women wanted to contribute something to help. They all sat down to discuss the details. Autumn was thrilled, she was sure they could raise the money for the kids. Some of them offered to bake, some offered to sew quilts, one women offered to make soap and candles to sell. Everything started to come together and so quickly. After the women met and made their plans they all left to get ready for the dance that night.

Time passed quickly that day and Austin arrived to pick up Autumn. She walked down the steps dazzling his eyes with her beauty.

"Austin...are you all right? Say something."

He shook his head trying to think of something to say.

"I am honored to have the pleasure of such a ravishing young woman on my arm tonight."

She smiled and tingled inside, taking her hand he leaned over to gently lay a kiss on the back of her hand. Then when he stood up he pulled flowers from behind his back.

"I can only say this bouquet pales next to you."

"Well aren't you a sweet talker, you look handsome yourself."

He offered her his arm and on they went to the dance. Austin helped her up in the buggy, then he hopped up and looked at her again with a smile on his face. Then they were on their way to the dance. It was a beautiful night, the sky was filled with stars.

"So how do you like Anaconda so far?"

Autumn smiled and gazed at the sky.

"So far I think it's divine. What do you think?"

For a few moments he was quiet and into thought before he spoke.

"The people are great, they all seem more like family. Then there is one site that really catches my breath and the best reason of all for living here."

He looked at her and she asked him.

"What site might that be?"

"The one I'm looking at right now."

Austin could barely keep his eyes on the road always looking at her.

"You're so caring and understanding as far as I can tell. To me that makes you a very beautiful woman."

Autumn was fiddling with her dress and bag, she was feeling a little flustered.

"Sally really likes the music you play on your harmonica. You are very good."

All he could do was chuckle a bit.

"Well thank you, my uncle taught me when I was just a young-en. We were very close."

Austin had a sad look on his face.

"I'm sorry, did I say something wrong?"

"No, my uncle was a great man. He and my Aunt were both very good to me, they took care of me after my father left and my mother had a nervous breakdown."

Autumn felt awful.

"I'm sorry, let's talk about something else. Tonight should be a joyous time, not for sadness."

"You're right, well look at this! We're here. Shall we dance?"

He helped her down from the buggy.

"Before we go in, I heard about what you went through, maybe someday we can talk about things. Just not tonight."

Autumn smiled and nodded her head, then they walked into the dance together. The music was fleeting, the people were happy and dressed exquisitely. Everyone seemed to be enjoying themselves.

"Hey look, there's Victoria. Why don't you go see her and I'll get us some punch."

"Thank you Austin, I would love some punch."

Autumn walked over to Victoria and they talked for a bit.

"I think this will be a huge success don't you Autumn?"

"I think so, there are so many people here. Maybe the entire town."

The ladies giggled and were happy about the turnout. Logan, Noah and Ronnie all walked in, there were three ladies watching them. Ronnie went over to see his sister and see how well she is doing, or seems to be doing.

"You look beautiful little sis. This dance is a good idea."

Austin and Tim came over with some punch.

"Hey Ronnie, it's good to see you again."

"Same here, Logan and Noah are here somewhere. Well hope all of you have a good time. Enjoy your evening."

Her brother and cousins seemed to have found some female company. Tim and Austin asked the ladies if they would like to dance. For the rest of the evening that was all they did, and everyone was happy. It was good for everyone, forgetting their troubles for a night. The evening flew by and before anyone realized it the dance was over.

Austin and Autumn said good night to Tim and Victoria, the boys were all ready gone. On their way home Austin stopped at the lake where he Noah and Logan use to go swimming. The light from the moon reflecting on the lake, it was quiet and blissful.

"We came down here a lot, swimming and once we even made a raft."
"Really? That sounds like fun, good times."

He chuckled for a minute or two.

"Not really, see as soon as we stepped on the raft it fell apart. We weren't good at building things then, we did more swimming than anything. We sure did have fun trying though."

They both laughed and shared stories from when they were younger. Autumn told him about the times they went swimming at a different lake and swung from a rope from the ground into the water.

"Once Logan was under water and grabbed my foot. I let out such a scream, I was sure I was being eaten by some strange fish or something."

They shared stories and laughed, they really enjoyed each others company. Austin leaned over and kissed Autumn.

"Well...I think we should be getting back. It's getting late."

"I'm sorry, I shouldn't have..."

"No no, I had a delightful evening and I enjoy being with you. It's just tomorrow I have a busy day and it is getting late. Oh and I promised Sally I would make a special dinner for her for being so brave and getting help for Victoria and me, would you like to join us?"

"I would like that very much, thank you for including me." "Then shall we say for six?"

"I'll be there."

Austin pulled the buggy in front of the saloon then jumped down to help Autumn down. He walked her to the door and said goodnight. She went upstairs to her room and sat in her chair for a spell gazing out the window. Trying to organize her thoughts of things she needed to do. All of it was too much to think about tonight, she was exhausted and all she wanted to do was go to bed. Things will work out once she starts in the morning.

She changed then went to bed, as always saying good night to her parents.

"I know you both can hear me, the dance was wonderful. I love you both always. Good night."

No sooner did she say good night then she was asleep. Many thoughts were going through her head, mostly her life in Wyoming. The holidays, parties, outings, her childhood. Autumn hears something, she looks towards her window and sees her mother standing there wearing the dress she wore Christmas day.

"Mom! Is it really you?"

"Yes sweetheart it is, you looked beautiful tonight at the dance. Your hair was perfect, you didn't need me."

Autumn couldn't believe she was talking to her mother.

"Mom your wrong, I do need you."

When she started to get out of bed her mother told her to stop.

"Mom I want to hug you."

"I have to go now, you're doing fine. I'll always love you. So will your father. Good night."

She blew a kiss to Autumn then she was gone. Autumn was struggling and she cried out for her mother not to leave. That moment she found herself sitting in bed, looking out the window realizing it was just a dream. Laying back down in bed she cried herself back to sleep. The night seemed long like it would never end. Autumn was wakened by a loud crack of thunder, she sat up in her bed breathing heavy it startled her so much. When she looked out the window the rain was pouring down.

"Oh no, this will delay building the orphanage."

She looked at the clock, it was still early, laying back down to collect her thoughts and plan for the day. Stew sounded perfect for a day like today. A large pot to take to the church for the children would be good for them. Victoria could bake some bread to go with the stew. Thoughts of her mother came back to her, it was only a dream but she did get to see her again. If only she could have hugged her, but that could never happen.

Autumn got out of bed to get ready, even if it was a little early she could take her time and try to relax. When she opened her closet door and bent over to reach for her shoes there was a small black box sitting there. She picked it up to open it and found earrings that belonged to her mother, her father gave them to her on their wedding night. She thought they were lost, but how did they get in her closet?

"Ronnie must have put them here to surprise me. He's so sweet."

How nice it was to have those earrings, she picked them up and put them away in her jewelry box in her drawer for safe keeping. As soon she was ready Autumn went downstairs to start working in the kitchen. Victoria came through the door.

"Good morning. The dance was wonderful last night don't you agree?"

Autumn looked at her shivering a bit and poured her a cup of hot coffee.

"Yes it certainly was. It's been a while since I enjoyed myself so much. Here have some coffee, it will help warm you."

Victoria thanked her, then went on to talk about the delay in building the orphanage due to the rain.

"Yes, unfortunate. I was thinking today would be a good day for making stew with your homemade bread Tim told me about. He said you bake bread better than anyone he knows. I thought it would be great to take to the children at the church. Would you mind?"

"Not at all. I'll make extra, I think we may have customers today and you can take some to your brother and cousins if you like?"

"I'm sure they would appreciate that. Thank you."

Victoria made breakfast for them and sat and talked about how their day would work out, then they went to work baking and cooking. Kneading the dough, chopping vegetables and cutting the beef, Things were starting to smell so good.

"Victoria, would you mind if I went to Noah's house to see my brother, I won't be long? I need to ask him something? Will you be good to take care of things here?"

"I 'll be fine, you go on don't worry about things here."

Autumn thanked her and promised not to be long. She grabbed her shawl to cover her head and went up the road to see Ronnie, Noah saw her coming and had the door open for her to come inside.

"Hey honey, what brings you here?"

"I came to see Ronnie, I need to talk to him. Is he awake?" Ronnie came into the room hoping nothing was wrong.

"Yes, I'm awake, is something wrong?"

"No nothing wrong. I just wanted to thank you." Ronnie looked baffled.

"Thank me! For what?"

"Because you left mom's earrings in my closet for me to find. The ones dad gave her on their wedding night."

Still he looked lost and had not a clue as to what she was talking about.

"I didn't leave anything in your closet, I thought you had them all along."

"What? Stop ribbing me, you had to put them there, I thought they were lost forever."

They both looked at each other astonished.

"If you didn't put them there then how did I get them?"

"Are you sure you didn't pack them and maybe forgot."

"I swear, I thought they were gone forever."

Noah looked at both of them.

"Maybe a ghost put them there, we have stories about such happenings in this town you know."

Autumn and Ronnie looked at him chuckling. Ronnie looked at Noah.

"A ghost, really? Now look who's ribbing who."

Only Autumn wasn't so sure, she did see her mother last night. At least it seemed real. She couldn't tell either of them about that.

"Well anyway I have them now. Victoria is baking bread and I'm cooking stew, you both have to stop over for dinner, bring Logan with you. See you all then."

She left closing the door behind her and feeling curious and bizarre, Ronnie didn't put them there so could her mother have left them? Was she dreaming last night? She would probably never really know, but it was wonderful to have her mothers earrings.

Autumn walked in the saloon and sitting at the table was a young woman.

"Hi, may I help you?"

The young woman turned and looked at Autumn.

"Hey, my name is Cora, is Marsha here? I'd like to talk with her if that's okay. She promised me a job here if I came back to town."

"Oh, well I'm sorry Marsha moved to Texas. She sold me this place."

Cora dropped her head in disappointment.

"Oh, I see. Well thank you anyway."

Cora turned to walk out the door.

"Wait don't go, please. Sit down I'll bring you some coffee."

"I don't want to trouble you."

"Have a seat, it's no trouble. Are you hungry? We have muffins made fresh this morning."

Cora was hungry, she traveled a long way.

"I would love a muffin, thank you."

Cora traveled from Hot Springs South Dakota. She had gone back there to marry her childhood sweetheart. Autumn was curious about her so they talked for a while.

"So Cora, that is a lovely name. Tell me about yourself."

She sipped some coffee to wash down the muffin before she spoke.

"Well I used to work for Marsha, until my boyfriend back home wrote to me asking me to marry him. We had a fight and I wasn't sure if I wanted to marry him or not. When I talked things out with Marsha she made me realize we would have days like that and if we wanted things to work out we would have to work hard for it, I thought about it but I reckon I took too long. When I finally went back home he was ready to hitch up with someone new. He told me he couldn't wait for me to make up my mind." Autumn felt terrible for her.

"I'm so sorry.'

"Thank you, anyway Marsha told me if things didn't work out I could come back here and she would hold my job for me."

Thinking about everything Cora told her and what Marsha did for her, hiring this woman would be a favor to Marsha even though she wasn't there. She did plenty for her, this is a way to help Cora.

"Well I'll tell you what, if Marsha said she would hold your job for you then you're hired. She helped me too, I want to return the favor. When can you start?"

Cora smiled so hard she nearly was in tears.

"I can start right away! Thank you so much."

After Cora was done with her muffin and coffee, Autumn poured her one more cup and invited her into the kitchen to help. Victoria was glad to see her again but sorry about how things turned out.

"I remember Marsha saying she may have to move back to Texas, I never thought it would be so soon. She's a great woman."

Autumn agreed even though she didn't know her or long. The storm wasn't easing up any, who knows when the town will be able to rebuild the building. Since Autumn and Ronnie moved to Anaconda there has been one thing after the other, so much excitement of just about any kind.

"Miss Snyder..."

"Please Cora, call me Autumn."

"Yes miss...Autumn. I was just wondering if you would mind if I went to the hotel to rent a room. I won't be gone long." Autumn smiled and shook her head.

"No need for a hotel room, there's a room upstairs, you can take that one."

Cora thanked her for her kindness, she started to wash the dishes while Victoria was ready to bake the bread. The stew was simmering and the smell of the kitchen was heavenly.

"Autumn, Victoria was telling me your making stew to send to the church for the children? Well if it's all right I'd like to make a small sweet for after their meal. I use apples to make them with, would you mind?"

"Not at all thank you so much for your offer. I'm sure they will appreciate that."

The woman work together very well, things were going smoothly.

"Well I promised the my brother and cousins that I would take them some lunch, I won't be long."

Victoria had some bread sliced and Cora had the apples ready, each one packed up what they made to send with Autumn. While she was gone the two women cleaned he kitchen and was packing food to take to the church. Victoria tried some of the apples Cora made.

"These are so good, where did you learn to make these?"

"It's nothing really, my grandmother taught me how to make these when I was knee high to a pony. That's how my grandfather said that."

They talked till Autumn came back getting to know each other better. Everyone in Anaconda had an interesting story to tell. Maybe that's why everyone was so close. The thunder hadn't eased any, Autumn was sure the children were scared. When she came back to the saloon the three women carried the food over to the church. They walked in and Father Morgan was tending to a little boy who was crying. Cora went over to ask why he was crying.

"I'm afraid he's scared of the thunder."

Cora remembered what that was like. As a little girl she was afraid also, until her grandmother told her a story about the thunder.

"Father may I please talk to him? I think I can help him."

"Of course, I hope you can. His name is Billy."

Cora reached down and tapped him on his shoulder.

"Billy I know you're afraid of the thunder, I use to be scared too when I was your age."

He looked up at Cora.

"You were?"

"I sure was, until my grandmother told me a story about thunder."
"What story?"

She sat down and put Billy on her lap.

"Well here's what my grandma told me. Up in heaven there are angels. When it gets cold they make a campfire to keep warm. So when ever you hear the loud thunder, That is an angel chopping down a tree and the loud noise it makes is the noise of the tree hitting the ground. It's really nothing to be scared of, the tree won't fall down from the sky. It just makes a noise when it falls." "Really? I didn't know angels get cold."

"Sure they do, just like we do. So when you hear that loud noise it's just the angels trying to keep warm."

At that moment there was a crack of thunder.

"Hey, they chopped a tree and it didn't fall all the way down here."

"Of course not. See, there's nothing to be scared of."

Billy looked up and said to the angels.

"You can chop as many trees as you want to stay warm. Right Miss Cora."

Cora looked at him and smiled.

"That's right Billy. Are you all right now?"

"I sure am."

Billy looked at Father Morgan.

"Father Morgan, can we send them some trees in case they run out? I don't want the angels to get cold."

He smiled and explained to Billy.

"Heaven will never run out of trees."

"Oh good. Now they will keep warm too."

Father Morgan looked at Cora and thanked her for her help, and the others as well for the food. Autumn looked around for Sally.

"Father, I don't see Sally."

"Here I am, I'm all cleaned up for supper. May I go now Father?"

"Of course you may Sally. Behave yourself."

"I will, right Miss Autumn?"

"She's always a joy, I've never had a problem with her. Thank you for letting me have time with her I do appreciate this."

Father nodded, he was happy to let her spend time with Sally. They all left the church together and Autumn made sure Sally was covered under her jacket. Autumn told Cora and Victoria she and Sally were going to stop at the general store and then they would go straight to Noah's to start supper, she thanked them again for their help with the food for the children.

"Sally we have to pick up a few things then we can go to cook your special dinner."

Sally was so exited she could hardly wait.

"Will Mr Austin be there too?"

"Yes he will, he wanted to be there and be a part of your celebration."

"Oh boy!"

When they walked into the general store the owner walked over to Sally when he saw Sally come in with Autumn.

"Well hello there little lady, I heard something nice about you and because you were such a brave little lady you can pick out anything in the store you want."

"Oh wow, Miss Autumn did you hear that?" "I sure did, go on and pick something."

It warmed their hearts to see Sally so happy and looking around the store to pick whatever she wanted. When she found something she brought it back to the owner to ask if what she picked would be ok to keep.

"Are you sure you want another doll?"

"Yes sir, Amelia needs a sister. I'll call her Nelly."

"I see, her sister Nelly, well I think that is dandy. Very good choice."

Autumn was smiling and reminded Sally to thank him.
"Thank you so much."

"Well you're very welcome."

Autumn had picked out what she needed, paid for them then she and Sally were on their way to the house. When they walked outside the rain had finally stopped, Sally looked up in the sky and saw a rainbow.

"Miss Autumn look, a rainbow. Look at the pretty colors."

"A rainbow means good luck. Something nice is supposed to happen."
"Something nice did happen, Amelia got a new sister."

Autumn giggled and agreed, then they walked to Noah's house and went inside.

"Hey ya all, Sally and I are here."

Ronnie walked in the room to greet them.

"Noah went to Logan's office, he'll be right back."

"Is anything wrong?"

"No, he just wanted to remind Logan about supper tonight. So Sally, I see you have a new doll."

"Yes, she's Amelia's new sister. The man at the store said I can pick out anything I wanted for being brave."

Ronnie picked her up with both her dolls in her arms.

"Well he's right, you are very brave and I didn't get to thank you. You saved my sister, Autumn."

"You're welcome. I love Miss Autumn too, I'll bet she would make a great mommy someday."

"Ok you stay here and play with your dolls and I'll go start supper."

Sally sat on the chair telling her dolls a story about when she and Autumn went shopping, and swimming and how Autumn helps people.

"Oh and everyone in town is helping to build us a new home. Well it's not a real home, a real home has a mommy and a daddy. Maybe someday we can get one of those."

Sally started singing to her dolls the same song Autumn sang to her. Ronnie excused himself to get some coffee.

"Sally would you like a glass of milk or juice?" "Thank you but no, I'll wait for supper."

Ronnie smiled at her then went to the kitchen and told Autumn the story she told to her dolls.

"She actually said that? About a real home!"

"She did."

This made Autumn think, is this what the other children are thinking also? It's sad. She went on cooking but this thought never left her mind. There was a knock at the door, Ronnie said he would get it, he opened the door and there was Austin.

"Well hey, come on in and sit down."

"Thank you. Hey Sally, I see you have two dolls now?"

"Yes sir, the man at the general store said I was brave and he told me to pick out anything I wanted for being brave. I thought Amelia needed a sister, so now we have Nelly."

Austin smiled at her.

"Well you're right, now Amelia will have a mommy and a sister. That was good thinking."

Ronnie watched as she lay her dolls on the chair and covered them with a blanket.

"It's there nap time now, we have to be quiet."

"Ok we will."

Ronnie gave Sally a picture book to look at while he took Austin in for some coffee and to see Autumn. They told him the story she told her dolls.

"That poor sweet girl." Autumn looked at Austin.

"Well hopefully this supper for her will make her feel better, I never thought about what those children think, now I know."

Austin nodded his head peaking in on Sally then turned back to Autumn.

"It must be hard for her, but I do believe you are making a difference in her life. I see how happy she is when she's with you. That has to help somehow."

"Well I have to finish up so would you two mind going in and keep an eye on her? I'll let you know when I'm through."

Noah came back from Logan's office and asked Ronnie and Austin to step outside

"Hey Sally, remember me?"

"I sure do, you're Mr. Noah. Hey"

"We'll be out here talking just a few minutes then we'll be right back in, will you be ok?"

"Yes Mr. Noah, I have to watch my babies."

The men stepped outside, since Sally';s babies were sleeping she decided to ask Autumn if she could help.

"Miss Autumn, my babies are sleeping. Can I help you?"

"I'd like that, would you carry this basket to the table please? That would be a big help."

Sally carried a basket and Autumn was behind her with dishes of food. She taught Sally how to set a table, and help out with smaller things.

"Well Supper is ready, would you mind calling the men in so we can start supper?"

"Oh boy, I sure will."

Sally went to the door and told the men supper was ready, by that time Logan had joined them on the porch.

"Hey Mr. Logan, are you eating with us?"

"I'd like that if you don't mind. After all this supper is for you."

"Oh yes, please eat with us."

They all chuckled, Logan said he would stay picked up Sally and carried her inside. Everyone sat down and Logan said grace. After grace Noah asked Sally if it was all right to start eating.

"Yes, dig in and let's eat."

Everyone loved Sally, you just couldn't help it, and Autumn was becoming more attached every time she was with her. Everybody enjoyed supper then after they finished Austin told Sally he would play a special song for her on his harmonica.

"Oh boy, let me wake up my babies so they can hear too."

They all gathered around while he played a song, Sally was so happy she looked as though she would bust. The evening was going very well and everyone had a great time, but now

Sally had to go back to the church. Autumn cleaned up the kitchen, Logan was leaving to go and Ronnie and Noah were ready to turn in themselves. Autumn and Austin walked Sally to the church and hugged her good night.

Austin walked Autumn back to her room but she seemed distant.

"Something is wrong, I can tell."

"You're right, something is wrong. Did Ronnie tell you what Sally said tonight? About a real home and a mommy and daddy?"

He knew and felt disturbed by it himself.

"Yes he did. It's terrible a little girl that age would think of something like that."

"If she's thinking like that what must the other children think?"

By the time they finished that talk they were standing in front of her door.

"Think of it this way, you know you can't do for all those kids, but you are helping Sally. I know that's not easy because I know you're heart. Even if just one child has someone, and she does have you and I know you have her. The whole town can see what I do. That's something."

She knew what he meant.

"I know you're right, well good night. Thank you for coming it meant a lot to Sally."

"If there is anything I can do, please let me know."

Autumn reached up and kissed him good night, thanking him once more then went in for the night.

Chapter 4

It was a beautiful morning, the sun was shining and hopefully it will dry the ground quickly so the men can resume building again. Women were coming to the saloon with many items. Autumn greeted them and saw the bountiful things they brought.

"Please come in, my my what treasures you all brought!"

75

Autumn had the women follow her to the store room. They brought canned goods, quilts, items for the auction. Everyone is so generous and it is for a good cause.

> "Oh my, ladies I appreciate everything you brought and all your help. I can't thank you enough."

Victoria walked in the store room.

> "Autumn, Tim's friend said he will let us use two of his pony's for pony rides for the children."

> "That is wonderful, look at the treasures these ladies brought! We're getting off to a fabulous start. Ladies thank you so much."

One of the ladies told her there was more to come. They weren't finished yet. Autumn was very appreciative of the women. When the ladies left she closed the door and locked it so they were safely tucked away.

> "The biggest thing we do need is a place to have this fair."

> "I'm sure we'll find something."

Autumn was pleased that things were working out so well. Victoria, Cora and Autumn sat down with a cup of coffee to talk about the details.

> "So far we have pony rides, a clown with balloons, a stand for baked goods and one for canned goods and quilts."

Cora was listening and she had joined in on the plans.

> "I know someone who could build a platform for the auction.

> He can get some chairs and put it all together, will that help?"

> "It most certainly will thank you."

Everyone in town was involved one way or another to take care of the children. Ronnie and Noah had been talking about what Ronnie would do now since he's moved to Anaconda.

> "I want to have my own ranch with horses and cattle, everything."

> "Well I know where you can buy a ranch and start with maybe a couple of horses, it would be a start till you can get to where you want to be."

That is Ronnie's dream, maybe now he can make that dream come true.

> "There is a ranch that's been up for sale for maybe a month now. It's not in the best shape but not the worse either. A little hard work and it could be a spectacular place. Because it could use some fixing up the man is selling it at a low price. Since we can't work on the orphanage until the ground dries up, why don't we take a ride out and have a look? See what you think."

Ronnie was more than ready, he and Noah hopped on the wagon and went to have a look at the ranch.

> "Why is he selling for such a low price? Does it need that much work?"

> "No, he has no way to repair the place and doesn't have the money to make the repairs. He's had the ranch for a very long time and now he just wants to relax in his old age. Can't really blame him for that."

> "No I guess you can't."

They were riding up to the ranch, Ronnie could see what the place looked like. Really it wasn't too bad at all. It's not too big but not too little, this is just what Ronnie was hoping for. They rode up in front of the door then went to talk to the owner, Hank Jenkins. Ronnie and Noah went to the door and knocked.

"Hey Mr. Jenkins, remember me? Noah from town?"

He looked at him for about a minute before he remembered.

> "Oh yeah, your brother is Logan, the doctor."

> "That's right, this is my cousin Ronnie. He and his sister just moved here from Wyoming, he may be interested in buying your ranch."

> "Well hello there young fella, pleased to meet you. Come in, come in."

Mr. Jenkins showed them around and let them walk around the ranch grounds. He was honest about the repairs needing tended to, Ronnie appreciated that. The house needed repairs but in Ronnie's eyes it was perfect. He could see in his mind exactly how he wanted everything.

> "Well Noah, do you think he's serious about the buying."

Noah looked at Ronnie's face, he saw that I'm in love look and he knew Ronnie wouldn't be able to resist.

"Mr. Jenkins, I believe he will be buying."

Mr Jenkins was hopeful but not sure. No one who has seen the ranch was interested. Ronnie walked over towards them, here it comes for sure Mr. Jenkins thought.

"Mr Jenkins, you just sold yourself a ranch."

He was dazed, he really said he would buy the ranch.

"Well now son, are you sure?"

"I am unless you'd rather I didn't buy?"

Suddenly he was struck with joy, shaking his hand he was ready to go in and sign the papers. Ronnie promised he would have the money for him the next day. That was good enough for Mr. Jenkins, he knew Logan and Noah a long time and Ronnie being their cousin he knew he could trust him.

"Thank you so much son, you don't know what joy you brought to me,
if there is anything you need please let me know. Bless you."

"Mr Jenkins, you brought me enormous joy, thank you."

Noah and Ronnie headed back home, the sun was shining brighter than ever, or maybe it was just Ronnie thinking that. Things are looking up for him and his sister.

"When you're ready to pick up some horses w can go to Philipsburg,
they have the best horses there and reasonably priced. That's where
the men around here buy there horses."

"Just as soon as I fix the fence around the barn, I'll be ready."

They just got back into town, the ground was beginning to dry.

"Look at that Noah, if the rain holds off we can start back to work on
the orphanage."

"Sure looks it, the sun dries the ground pretty fast. Maybe even
tomorrow."

Autumn was open for regular business since the work was stopped because of the rain.

Ronnie and Noah walked in, Logan had stopped in, Austin was there and a couple of men who were helping to build the orphanage.

> "I have some great news, the plans for the fair are coming along fine, you should see the treasures some of the women in town brought for the auction and for the booths. I'm just beside myself!"

This was no surprise for Logan and Noah, they've lived in this town a very long time and they knew the people and how everyone pulls together when needed.

> "As soon as we have a place to hold the fair I can have the posters printed up to hang."

Ronnie and Autumn were so pleased. Autumn was feeling generous.

> "Hey ya all, drinks for everyone, on me."

There was a cheer that filled the saloon with festive joy. Cora came downstairs to help serve drinks. She looked so much different dressed like a saloon girl but that is her job. A maroon colored skirt and white blouse with black fishnet stockings with a cowgirl hat and heels. Cora was partial to cowboy style hats, not the usual feather hat like other saloon girls wore.

Austin went over to Autumn to talk.

> "Hey beautiful, I say later we pick up Sally and go on a picnic, what do you say?"

> "I'd love to and I know Sally would too."

Father Morgan never came into a saloon before but today he did.

> "Miss Snyder, I know you would never see me in here but this is important. Sally is very upset, she won't talk to anyone. She's crying and none of the other children know why. Do you have some time to come over and see her?"

Autumn was worried, Austin said he would go with her.

> "Of course, right now. Cora would you handle things till I get back?"

> "You don't have to ask, go on."

Austin and Autumn rushed over to the church, they found Sally crying in the back, last pew. They each sat on opposite sides of her with their arms around her.

"Sally sweetie, what's wrong?"

"Nelly ran away, she's gone. I put them to bed together but when I woke up she was gone."

Austin and Autumn looked at each other then he talked to Sally.

"Are you sure she's not here somewhere, playing maybe?"

"No no, I can't find her."

Autumn asked Father where she slept and he took her there.

"Autumn searched all around, she couldn't find her. Then as she was leaving the room she noticed the door wouldn't open all the way, when she looked behind it there was Nelly. Autumn picked her up then started to leave the room when another little girl was standing there. Her name was Liza.

"I'm sorry, I didn't mean to make Sally cry. Her doll was so pretty and I don't have one. I wanted to play with her a little bit, then Sally woke up I just put her behind the door and ran."

Autumn felt bad for the girl. These poor children need more in their lives.

"Well I do understand but don't you think it would have been polite to ask Sally if you could play a while with her?"

"I guess so."

"Let's go tell her where Nelly was, okay?"

Liza agreed and she went with Autumn to tell Sally what she did. Sally was so happy to see Nelly she told Liza they could both play with them together. Father Morgan thanked Autumn and Austin. Austin had an idea.

"Hey you two, Autumn and I were talking a while ago, how would you both like to go with us on a picnic later? You can both come and bring Amelia and Nelly with you. Would you like that?"

The girls were so excited and couldn't wait to go. Liza looked at Father Morgan. "Would that be okay, please?"

He looked at the two girls and agreed they could go. Autumn told Father they would be over later to pick them up. Austin walked Autumn back to the saloon.

"Austin that was so sweet of you."

"It was nothing. I have something to do before we go then I'll be over to pick you up. See ya later."

He kissed her on the cheek and rushed off.

"Hey ya all, how is everything?"

Cora had everything running smoothly, everyone was in good spirits. That was the best site in a while. Logan looked at Autumn, she seemed fine.

"Sweetie is everything good with Sally?"

"Yes they sure are, just a little misunderstanding. Austin and I are taking Sally and her friend Liza on a picnic later." Noah look baffled.

"Liza?"

"Yes, Sally's new doll was missing and Liza took it to play with while Sally was sleeping. When she was waking up Liza couldn't get the doll back so she put it behind the door. No harm, Sally felt better just getting Nelly back."

Ronnie smiled and shook his head.

"They're kids, they always settle things. Sometimes better than adults. So where is Austin?"

"I really don't know. He was in a rush. Well I better fix something to take on this picnic, see ya all later."

The boys left, Logan had patients to see, Ronnie was getting things together to settle up with Mr. Jenkins, and Noah had lumber to pick up for the orphanage. From the looks of the ground they would be ready to go back to work in the building the next day. Victoria and Autumn were cooking, not just for the picnic but for the supper crowd.

"So Autumn, not to pry but Austin seems sweet on you in a big way."

"Oh I don't know, I haven't really noticed."

Victoria knew he was, she has seen that look so many times before.

"So all of you are going on a picnic?"

"Yes, Sally was upset so he wanted to do something to cheer her up."

They continued to cook as they talked.

"Oh Autumn I almost forgot, some of the ladies brought more things for the fair, you should go take a peek. Beautiful things."

"I don't know about you but I think this fair will be a huge success."

Cora had walked in on the end of the conversation, Autumn is a special person doing so much for those kids.

"Autumn, I would like to make a donation for the orphanage."

"Thank you, what ever it is you can put it with the rest of the donations."

"No, not that kind of a donation."

Cora picked up her bag and pulled out an envelope.

"This is what I want to donate."

Autumn took the envelope and looked inside.

"Cora, this is a lot of money. Are you sure?"

Cora made a donation of fifteen hundred dollars.

"I'm sure, it has taken me a long time to save it and I can't think of a better way to put it to use."

Victoria saw serious in this conversation.

"Well if you two will excuse me I have an errand I have to run, would you mind Autumn?"

"No of course not."

Cora and Autumn gazed at each other. "Cora, why?"

"When I was a young girl not much older than Sally, my girlfriend lost her parents. She was put in an orphanage.

I used to visit her but she dreaded living there. The place caught fire and burned down, they got all the children out. Except for my friend. She didn't make it out. I couldn't help her but I can help these kids. Please take it, it would mean so much to me."

Tears were rolling down Cora's face, Autumn's eye's were filling with tears. She hugged Cora and they cried a few minutes together.

"I'm so sorry, that is tragic, but are you sure you want to donate all of this money?"

"I'm sure."

Cora was determined for Autumn to accept the money. "Thank you Cora, it will go to good use."

Autumn told Cora she would be right back, she wanted to give the money to Father Morgan. She rushed over to the church and went inside. Father was setting things up for Sunday's mass.

"Miss Snyder hello. I didn't expect to see you till later."

"Yes Austin and I will be back later but I'm here for a different reason. I wanted to give you this donation of fifteen hundred dollars. This is one donation I don't want to hang on to, it's from Cora for the orphanage. What ever is needed for the children."

"That is a lot of money, is she sure?"

"She is, please will you take it Father?"

"I would be happy to, it will be a great help. Will you thank her for me please?"

"I will, thank you and we'll be by later."

Autumn went back to the saloon and told Cora that Father thanked her, then they went back to cooking. There was a few of the towns men there to grab some grub. Cora told her she had fed them and gave them coffee, they were on their way out of town on business.

> "That's fine. You have been a great help, I can see why Marsha would have hired you back. You have a great business mind. How would you feel about keeping the books for me?"

> "Me? Really? I would love to thank you so much."

> "I've been watching you and your work with the business. It makes sense with your mind. It would be a waste not to have you keep the books."

Cora accepted, when she hoped to be hired back she never thought it would be to keep books, but she is appreciative. This worked out so much better than she had hoped. Noah came in, he was going out of town for a day or two and wanted to say good bye to Autumn.

> "I have some business to tend to so I'll see you when I get back. Logan is here and of course Ronnie."

> "What kind of business? Will you be all right?"

> "Don't worry, nothing bad but I can't say right now. See ya when I get back."

Noah left leaving everyone concerned, he didn't even tell Logan. Ronnie went to visit Mr. Jenkins to see if he needed any help.

> "I'm not trying to rush you out of here, I just thought you could use some help and I brought you the money."

> "Well thank you. I could use some help if you're sure you don't mind?"

> "Not at all, just lead me on."

Mr. Jenkins wasn't planning on taking everything, he was moving in with his son just a few ranches away. His son, Brent, was fully aware of the deal his father made.

> "My son will be here later today to take me home with him. I just wanted to pack up my clothes and some personal things if you wouldn't mind helping. That's the only way I can be ready in time."

Ronnie was more than willing to help. His son is very lucky to still have his father and must appreciate it to take him in, at least Mr. Jenkins will be well taken care of. He pointed out to Ronnie things he wanted packed and Ronnie would oblige.

"Mr. Jenkins, is this you and your wife?"

"Yes it is, she was a good woman. Kinds like her aren't easy to find. She gave birth to our son but didn't survive herself. My Emmy would have been a good mama. She was ill at the time she gave birth to Brent, we just weren't sure if either of them would make it, Brent did. I reckon I'm lucky to have my son. My heart broke when I lost her, I never remarried."

Ronnie felt sad for him, he apologized for bringing up a sad time but Mr. Jenkins didn't think he had, there were so many good years with her.

"That woman is still alive, right here in my heart. They never leave you son, you remember that."

Ronnie was thinking about his parents, thinking hard he realized Mr. Jenkins was right, he could feel the love from his parents in his heart. It was a great feeling. Soon they had finished packing in time for his son who just arrived to pick up his father.

"Hey pa! I'm here."

"Son, is that you?"

Brent walked in the kitchen where Ronnie was talking to Brent's father and sipping coffee.

"This is Ronnie, he bought the ranch. This is my son Brent."

"Nice to meet you."

"Nice to meet you Ronnie. Hope dad gave you a fair price."

"More than fair. Your father is a great man. It was great getting to know him in such a short time. I promise I'll take good care of the ranch."

Brent smiled and so did his father.

"No doubt, thank you for helping him. It's appreciated more than you know. Please feel free to stop by the ranch sometime, I'm just two ranches down. We'd love to have you."

Ronnie thanked him and helped Mr. Jenkins onto the wagon and waving as they rode away. Ronnie was looking around thinking about where to start first. Thinking aloud to himself.

"Well the fence would be a great place to start, if I'm going to have horses I'll need a fence."

Mr. Jenkins left some wood in the barn, Ronnie started right away. He was too excited about having his own ranch to put it off.

"Dad, hope you can hear me. I have my own ranch now. Just what I always wanted. Wish you could be here to see it, Autumn and I miss you and mom. I know what Mr. Jenkins meant when he said your loved ones will always be with you, I can feel you here right now."

Ronnie looked up in the sky, a rainbow appeared.

"I know that's you dad, thank you."

Ronnie went to work on the fence. When Ronnie went into the barn he found everything he needed. While he started working on the fence Autumn was back at the saloon packing a basket, then Austin walked in to pick her up, when she turned around she saw he has Sally and Liza with him.

"Well Miss Autumn, Liza and Sally are ready for the picnic, are you ready?"

She looked at the girls and smiled.

"I sure am, and I packed a feast. Shall we go?"

They walked out and Austin picked up the girls and put them in the back of the wagon then helped Autumn up in front.

"Well I feel special."

"Oh really? Why?"

"Simple my dear Miss Autumn, I'm going on a picnic with three of the pretties girls in town. I feel like the luckiest man in town."

They giggled and were about ready to leave when Austin turned around to give Liza a bag.

"Liza, before we leave you need to open this bag."

She took the bag and looked inside, suddenly she was excited.

"Sally look, I have babies too, almost like yours!"

"Hey they do almost look like mine."

"They are different so you two won't get your babies mixed up. Now
are we ready for a picnic?"

Everyone shouted yes, it was a beautiful day and great company. The sun was shining
and the sky was the bluest anyone has seen. After all the rain there was a fresh clean smell in
the air. Sally and Liza were playing with there dolls and giggling. Autumn looked at Austin.

"That was really a very sweet thing you did for Liza, for both girls."

"I just figured some time away would do them both good, us too."

"Austin, you are the sweetest man I've ever known, and the most
thoughtful."

It wasn't long before they arrived at the lake, Autumn had the girls change into their
swimsuits and she and Austin sat close by to watch them. They talked and got to know each
other more, the girls were having a great time splashing. The lake was surrounded by green
trees, the sun reflected off the lake and wild flowers were growing in some areas. Liza called
out to Sally.

"Sally look, it's a deer!"

"Shhhhh...not too loud. You'll scare him and he'll run away."

Autumn and Austin sat and giggled under their breath so the girls wouldn't hear them.
They were both so cute together. After about an hour or so Autumn called the girls out of the
lake to eat. Austin and Autumn wrapped towels around the girls, dried them off then they all
sat to enjoy their picnic. They all laughed and horsed around, it was a merry time for all of
them. When they finished eating they sat around Austin while he told stories. Autumn had
a smile on her face, she never met anyone like him. He truly cares about others, and seems
to love children. Everyone was having a great time, so great they never paid attention to the
time. The sun was just beginning to set, the horizon was painted beautiful shades of pink,
purple and some orange.

"Well I say we better head back home, Father Morgan is going to
wonder what happened."

No one really wanted to go but it was starting to get late. During the ride back to town the girls fell asleep in back of the wagon. A slight breeze was kicking in, Austin stopped the wagon and he and Autumn covered the girls with an extra blanket, then started again to head for home.

> "Thank you for a wonderful time, I know the girls enjoyed themselves as much as I did."

> "You're very welcome, I enjoyed watching them splashing in the lake and playing mommy."

Smiling at him they were soon back in town and stopped at the church, they each picked up a girl and their dolls and carried them inside. Austin apologized for keeping them out later than they intended but Father Morgan wasn't worried, he knew he could trust them with the girls. He thanked them both for taking them out and told them they would be welcome any time if they wanted to take them again.

Austin walked Autumn to her door, kissed her on the cheek and told her he would see her the next day. Autumn went into her room and saw a lily on her bed. How did it get there, that was her mother's favorite flower? Ronnie may have left it there, she would thank him tomorrow. Autumn put the lily in a single vase with some water and set it by her bedside, then quickly drifted to sleep.

The next morning when Autumn woke up the lily was missing from her vase, it was from her mother, she was sure of it now. She got out of bed and dressed for the day then went downstairs. In the kitchen were Cora and Victoria. They looked at each other then Cora poured some coffee and left the kitchen.

> "Where is she going?"

> "She is serving coffee to your brother."

> "He's here? I'll be right back."

> Victoria smiled and said to herself. "Maybe."

> "Ronnie, what are doing here so early?"

She knew something was up, he was smiling so big she thought he would bust.

> "I all ready spoke to Cora and Victoria, they are going to handle things here for maybe an hour while you come with me."

"What? What are you talking about I can't leave them to do all the work."

Cora looked at her.

"You just go with your brother, things will be fine here, bye."

Everyone was acting strange and she couldn't figure out why, but she went with Ronnie anyway. During their ride out to someplace Ronnie never spoke a word but Autumn was curious. Finally Ronnie spoke.

"There, straight ahead."

Autumn looked and saw a ranch that needed some work.

"That ranch up ahead? Not bad but it could use some work. So why did you bring me here?"

Ronnie still had that smile in his face.

"This is my ranch, I bought it yesterday." Autumn didn't know what to say.

"All of this is mine. Oh and I'll have it fixed up enough for you to have the fair here, if that meets your approval."

"You really bought this? Your serious about the fair being held here?"

Ronnie was laughing, she could barely talk.

"I'm very serious."

Autumn couldn't believe what was happening.

"I think we and the town are having some really good luck. Thank you so much."

She hugged Ronnie so tight he could barely breath.

"Rainbows really do bring good luck."

Ronnie looked at her strangely.

"What are you talking about?"

"Austin and I saw a rainbow, they are said to bring good luck, and it has."

Ronnie didn't mention the rainbow he saw, he took it as a message from their father, but she never told him about the lily their mother left for her. Those were their secrets.

"Ronnie mom and dad would be so proud of you."

"You too, you're running your own place of business." "Speaking of business I really should be getting back."

One more hug and Ronnie rode her back to the saloon.

"Here we are sis, have a good day I'll talk to you later." "Thank you. I'm happy you have your ranch."

He nodded and rode on to take care of some things. Just before she walked inside Logan had called out to her.

"Good morning Logan, how are things at with your patients?"

"Going well thank you, I was going to ask you the same thing." "Things just seem to be moving along. Thank you."

They were both in good spirits but Logan seemed to have something on his mind.

"Are you all right Logan? You seem like something is wrong?"

"Not really, I should be use to Noah going off with no reason, at least not saying why he has to leave, but I reckon I'm not."

Autumn gave Logan a hug.

"Tell me this, has he ever done this and not come back all right?"

She really made him think, that was a good question.

"I can't say he has."

"Having faith in someone, like this, isn't easy. Noah, like you, is a man now. I'm sure he'll be fine."

Logan smiled knowing she was right, he has never come back from these trips harmed.

"Thank you. How about I buy you lunch at the hotel?" "I would love that, I'll meet you there around noon?"

"See you then."

Autumn went inside and directly to the kitchen. Victoria couldn't wait any more.

"So how was your time with Ronnie?"

Cora and Victoria giggled.

"You both knew what this little ride was about?"

Cora looked and smiled at her.

"Well not completely but he did say he bought a ranch. How was it, how does it look?"

Autumn was excited about this.

"He bought the Jenkins ranch." Victoria was surprised.

"The Jenkins ranch, I hope Mr. Jenkins gave him a good price, that ranch needs some work. Not a great deal but still."

"Ronnie says he gave it to him for practically nothing and he doesn't mind fixing it up. He's all ready started, and the best part is he is going to fix up the barn part of the ranch as quickly as possible so we can hold the fair there."

The girls looked at her, Cora especially was excited.

"That would be so wonderful. Now we have a place we better think about getting the posters made."

"You're right, now that brings me to a question I have for Victoria. I have everything written down what I want on the posters and a list of things I need from the general store. Would you mind running these two errands for me please? I have some paper work I really need to tend to?"

She nudged Cora on the arm so she wouldn't say anything since she did ask her to keep the books.

"I'd be happy to."

Victoria looked over the list.

"This might keep me busy for a a short while, are you sure you want me to do this now?"

"Yes please, if you don't mind?"

"I don't mind one bit, be back as soon as I'm done."

"You don't have to rush, it will give you a break from the kitchen."

Victoria left curiously. Autumn peeked out the kitchen door to make sure she had left.

"She's gone, I sent her on the errands so we can talk. She and Tim are getting hitched and I told her I would take care of things, would you help me with the arrangements?"

"Heck yeah, I would be more than glad to help."

They sat at a table with paper and cups of coffee making plans. The wedding would take place at the church, Autumn worked that part out with Father Morgan. The wedding party would be at the saloon and that's where Cora would come in, helping to decorate and send out invitations.

"They will be living in Tim's house so that's one less thing."

Cora's eyes grew big.

"Have you seen his house? It's not very big nor small but so very nice. It's a medium ranch house like the one Ronnie just bought. They will be so happy, Tim was telling me she can redo the house anyway she wants, it will be their home not just his."

"How wonderful, Tim will make Victoria a great husband, he always thinks of her."

They sat there making plans before Victoria came back from the errands Autumn sent her on.

"This will be a beautiful celebration Autumn. You are so busy with planning the fair and this wedding, what about your life?"

"I don't know what you mean, I do have a life. Between Austin and Sally, we go out together. It's just right now these things need tended to, when it's all over I will have more time. They both know that. Besides Austin and I are just friends."

Cora looked at her.

"Does he know that? It seems to me he's wants to be more than just friends, by the looks on his face when he see's you."

"Of course he knows, it's just your imagination. Now we better finish this up, Victoria will be back soon."

They finished up and hid their papers then started to fix lunch. Victoria came in.

"Autumn, I just saw Logan and he said he would meet you for lunch shortly."

"Oh no, I almost forgot."

"Cora and I can finish up here, go on. I'll put these things in a box and set them aside so you can pick it up after lunch."

"Victoria thank you so much, I don't know what I would do without you and Cora. You both have been an enormous help. Thank you both."

With that being said Autumn rushed to meet her cousin at the hotel. Along the way she saw Tim Birescik.

"Good afternoon Mr. Biresck, how are you today?"

He tipped his hat to her.

"I'm very well thank you. How are you?"

"I'm well also thank you. I was wondering, do you know about when you and Victoria would be getting hitched? She may have told you I'm planning the arrangements and if you have a date in mind it would help with the planning."

"Yes she did mention that to me, you do know that really isn't necessary for you to go through all that trouble, especially when I know you're also working on the plans for the fair to raise money for the orphanage."

"Really it's no trouble at all."

"Well if you're sure. We hoped to be hitched next Saturday."

"Thank you very much, I'll have it all set up. Have a good day."

He wished her the same and went on his way. Autumn arrived at the hotel and saw Logan waiting for her.

"I'm sorry I'm late."

You're not that late, we're fine. They have a chicken plate that sounded so good, I ordered for the both of us but if you prefer something else..."

"No no, that sound delicious. Thank you."

All through their lunch they sat and talked about her planning the fair and the wedding, Ronnie buying a ranch and curious talk about Noah. So much seemed to be happening all at one time, not to mention rebuilding the orphanage.

"Did you see the men have the core of the building laid out, the ground is dry so work has begun again."

"I did notice that, if they keep up at that pace it should be done in no time."

Ronnie stopped in and saw they were having lunch. "Ronnie, what brings you here?"

"No offense Autumn but I heard about the lunch they are having here and wanted to try it for myself."

"No offense, I think you'll like it, it was excellent. Don't you agree Logan?"

"No doubt about that. Well Autumn thank you for joining me for lunch and I will see you both later."

"Thank you for lunch I did enjoy it very much as well as the company."

Autumn had to get back and told Ronnie she would also see him later. The plans for the wedding had to be moving fast. She went to let Father Morgan know what the date would be then rushed back to the saloon to help Victoria and Cora then work on getting things together. Time was going by quickly they were so busy, the dinner crowed came in, the three ladies tended to them and they were gone that fast.

"Thank you Victoria and Cora so much for your help today. I couldn't have done this without you. Everything is cleaned up and I'm closing up early tonight, I have so many things I have to take care of. I'll see you both in the morning, take care and thank you."

Cora looked at her and smiled.

"Are you sure, Victoria and I don't mind staying?"

"No that's fine, it's been a long day. See you both in the morning."

Victoria and Cora left to go to the general store to buy some things they needed, then went their separate ways wishing each other a good night. Autumn went up to her room to work on the plans for the wedding but was so tired she went right to sleep. There was a knock on her door, she sat up and asked who was there but no one answered. She looked out her window, it was night.

"Who could that be at this time of night?"

She went to the door cracked it open and nearly fainted. The man standing there grabbed her before she hit the floor and walked her over to the bed.

"Daddy, is it really you? It can't be."

"It is me, I had to come see you and tell you how proud I am of my little girl. Your mother and I are watching over you and Ronnie. You're both doing very well."

"We miss you both so much."

"We know that, and we know you're both in pain over this. Don 't let the pain ruin your lives, we'll be together again one day. Until then we want you both to be happy."

"The other night when I came to my room there was a lily on my bed, was that from mom?"

"It was, her way of saying we're keeping an eye out for you and Ronnie. I have to go now, we love you both."

With that being said he father faded away. Autumn sat straight up in her bed breathing heavily.

"Daddy, we love you too, tell mom we love and miss her also."

She walked over to the window gazing at the sky, it was filled with stars and a huge full moon. The night was clear and there was a gentle breeze whisking through. Tears filled her eyes as pain filled her heart. Still she felt like there was a blank part of her life she just couldn't recapture, she couldn't understand why. Autumn went to her bed, lay down and cried herself back to sleep.

The next morning she was in the kitchen early when Cora and Victoria walked in and saw her hard at work. Cora and Victoria looked at each other hoping she is all right.

"Autumn, honey is everything all right?"

"Oh, good morning. I'm sorry I didn't hear you come in, hope you both had a good night."

Cora walked over to her and repeated Victoria's question.
"Honey, Victoria and I are concerned, you are all right aren't you?" Autumn giggled.

"I'm fine really, I just felt this sudden burst of energy and needed to do something. So I came down and thought I would do some baking. Really there's nothing to be concerned about."

There wasn't much they could do but believe her. Soon they were all busy getting things set up for the day when there was a knock at the back kitchen door, Autumn froze for a brief moment and Victoria answered the door.

"Noah! Welcome home, we hope you had a safe trip."

"I did ladies thank you very much. Would you mind if I borrowed Autumn for a short spell, I promise to bring her back."

The ladies both said yes and Noah took Autumns hand leading her out the door and over to Logan's office where Ronnie was waiting with Logan.

"Thank you for sparing me some time, I have something important to tell the three of you. It has to do with my trip."

They looked at each other not knowing if they should worry or not.

> "Relax it's nothing bad. As you know the town has been in need of a sheriff, well a few days ago I received a telegram from the Attorney General Sheriff. He is in Great Falls on business. He wanted to talk with me so I had to go to him. The business had to do with a sheriff for our town, so he appointed me Sheriff of Anaconda. I wasn't sure if I would be the one to get this job, but I did. That's why I never said anything before I left."

They were all excited for Noah and could hardly believe the news. Autumn went over to him and kissed him on the cheek.

> "This can be a dangerous job, are you sure this is what you want?"

Ronnie put his hand on her shoulder.

> "Autumn, it's not any more dangerous than bounty hunting. He'll be a great sheriff."

> "Here here."

Said Logan. Autumn knew what Ronnie said was right, and this would keep him closer to home instead of roaming off to just anywhere.

> "Noah, we're all very proud of you."

Logan stepped over to say his words to Noah.

> "If mom and dad were here, they would be so proud they would probably bust."

Noah was excited about all this.

> "Thank you all so much. Now I just need to find myself a deputy."

> "Noah, before I forget I planned a wedding for Victoria and Tim, Saturday. They know I'm planning but that's all they know. Will you be able to attend, please?"

> "Count on me, I'll be there."

As the days went by Autumn and Cora were working on the wedding plans, the women in town would bring items for the fair and the men worked on building the orphanage. Things were coming along smoothly, when finally, Saturday, the wedding has arrived. Everything was even more beautiful than she had anticipated, Cora's eyes watered up and when Autumn looked at her she shook her head. "Cora are you all right? Take out, save that for the wedding."

Cora giggled some then dried her eyes.

> "I just can't help myself, this all turned out so beautiful. You planned a beautiful wedding."

Autumn looked at her and offered her a kerchief.

> "Listen, I did have some help you know, you were a big part of this don't forget."

> "All I did was follow your instructions, you made all this happen."

Autumn put her arm around Cora then they went to get dressed for the wedding. Everyone would go to the church for the ceremony then to the saloon for the party. The way the place was decorated you would never know it was a saloon from the inside. Austin met the two ladies at the saloon and then went together to the church.

> "Well darned of I'm not the lucky one to have two such beautiful escorts for the hitch-en. Shall we go ladies?"

Austin offered an arm to each lady then left for the church. People were filling up the seats and the music was playing till everyone was in place. Tim came out and stood at the alter, the signal was given that Victoria was ready and the wedding song was being played. Everyone turned to watch Victoria start her walk down the aisle. She was so beautiful, orange blossoms lightly swept across her dress, a symbol of happiness and fertility. The groom, Tim, looked just as handsome and a bit nervous yet smiling.

Victoria reached the alter and Tim took her hand, they turned to Father to begin the ceremony. After they spoke their vows to each other all the children lined up to sing the new bride and groom a song. When the ceremony was over everyone went to the saloon for the party. There was music, dancing and plenty of food. Tim and Victoria pulled Autumn aside for a short spell.

> "Victoria and I wanted to thank you for all you've done for us, so we have a little something for you."

Autumn opened the package carefully and quickly as possible.

"A book, Wuthering Heights. I've heard about this book, it's very popular from what I understand. Thank you both so much, it really wasn't necessary."

"It was to us, you have done so much for Victoria and me, you took care of her while I was gone. We want to show our appreciation." They all smiled and hugged each other.

"You certainly have done that, now go and enjoy yourselves, this is your night."

They all sat down for dinner, conversation and gaiety filled the room. Austin stood up to speak.

"May I please have everyone's attention. Won't you join me in a toast to the newly married couple, a perfect couple. May they find much happiness and love in their journey together. A blessing mto their life and may it be as perfect as they are as husband and wife. Take care of each other and be happy. Blessings to you both."

Everyone raised their glasses and repeated, blessings. After dinner the group of men played music and it was now time to cut the cake. It was a beautiful cake that also had little orange blossoms. The bride and groom cut the first piece then Autumn and Cora cut the remaining cake for the guests. Everyone was having a great time, relaxing and eating, dancing. The party went on till almost eleven that night before people started leaving for home. Mr. and Mrs. Tim Birescik left hand in hand, he helped her up to the wagon, Austin, Autumn and Cora had the wagon loaded with their wedding gifts and stood there with Ronnie, Noah and Logan waving good bye.

They said good night to each other and Cora and Autumn went inside.

"I'll help you clean up Autumn."

"No, what you're going to do is go upstairs and get some rest. I'll see you in the morning, this will hold until then."

"Are you sure?"

"Go on, have a good night."

Autumn called to Noah before he walked too far away, he came back.

"Is something wrong?"

"No everything is fine, I just wanted to congratulate you again and I'll see you in the morning sheriff."

Autumn looked around after Cora and Noah left, this would be too much for one morning. Maybe she would do some of it tonight. At the least gather the dishes and take them to the kitchen, maybe even empty the trash, then locked up for the night. Now she was so exhausted she could barely climb the stairs, but she did. It was a little warm that evening so she opened her window for some fresh air while she slept. The night was quiet, the crickets were chirping. So peaceful and a good kind of tired in a relaxing way. Autumn lay in bed gazing out the window for a while, it was a beautiful night. Soon her eyes became heavy and she couldn't keep them open, so she drifted off into a deep sound sleep.

Ronnie stayed at his ranch, even though there was repairs needed, it wasn't so bad he couldn't live there. He wasn't very tired so he sat on the porch for a while picturing in his head how things will be once he makes all the repairs, it will be what he's always dreamed about. He imagined horses in the barn and running around in the gated area he is working on now. Maybe paint the house and the barn, all these ideas gave him something to work for. He looked up in the sky talking.

"Well dad, my dream will come true, I only wish you could be here to see it and share it with me. Maybe...maybe you and mom can see it now. Autumn and I will be fine, we miss you both so much. We love you. Good night."

He went inside to turn in for the night, he felt somehow they could hear him, that was all that mattered.

The next morning the rooster was crowing as the sun rose, Ronnie woke up and looked out the window.

"Hey Rowdy, keep it down will you? I'd like to sleep a little longer."

Ronnie shut the window an went back to bed, last night was a long night and he earned that much. Noah was up and at his office, he wanted to fix things up his way. Never did he ever think he would be a sheriff, he was use to bounty hunting. Logan stopped in to see him, he had no patients to see today.

"So what are you going to do with no patients." Logan thought a moment.

"Maybe I'll go fishing, it's been a while since I've done any fishing. I don't reckon you would be available to go with me?"

"Sorry I can't today. I have things here to get done, there's a lot here to go through. See what I need and don't need. This place could use a good sweep and dusting."

"Well ok then, I'll catch you a fish after I catch one for me."

Noah laughed while Logan looked at him wondering what he was laughing about.

"I remember the last time we went fishing, you couldn't catch the bait much more than a fish." Logan looked so seriously at him.

"Here's five dollars that says I can, two of them." "Why not make it ten, doctor?"

"Ten it is, hold your supper till I bring that fish home." "Hold supper? I better pack a lunch."

Noah couldn't help but laugh which made Logan all the more determined to catch those fish.

"You'll be laughing when you're eating fish, wait and see."

Logan left leaving Noah laughing and getting on with his work. He went to his wagon to make sure he had everything he needed, then he was on his way to the lake. Autumn had stepped outside for a moment and saw Logan driving by, they waved at each other then she went back inside. The fishing hole he was going to wasn't very far from where Ronnie lives, he was thinking about stopping by to see if he would like to go with him. It was a great day for fishing, he Noah and Ronnie use to go when they were kids. Logan was thinking about all the times they had together when they were kids.

It wasn't long when he was pulling into Ronnie's ranch, he was outside working on the fence by the barn. One look and you could see he was putting his all into the repairs needed.

"Morning Logan, what brings you out this way? Not that I mind, it's always good to see you."

"I was just passing by and thought I would stop and see if you would like to join me in some fishing?"

Ronnie thought a moment, it would be nice but he does have a lot of repairs to get done.

"I don't know, I have plenty of work around here to get done. I promised Autumn she could hold the fair here, the auction in the barn, and I need to get this fence fixed for the pony rides."

Logan looked around, he was off for the day and would be more than happy to help Ronnie. Two could get the job done quicker than one.

"Tell you what, you go fishing with me now and after I'll help you with what you need to get done. With two of us it will go quicker and easier. What do you say?"

Ronnie was thinking and looking at the fence, it would be easier with two working on the repairs.

"You got yourself a deal."

Ronnie went in the house to get his fishing rod and was back out and hopping on the wagon with Logan. The time he would be fishing with Logan they could easily make up and then some. Along the way they talked about old times they spent together and laughing about some of the things they did, teasing Autumn, pulling pranks, and stealing pies after they're mother's baked them for Sunday suppers.

"So why didn't Noah come along?"

"He's at his office cleaning things up, getting organized."

"Oh yeah, our new sheriff. Remember how we used to talk about what our lives would be like when we grew up? How different they are since then, how things have changed."

Logan saw his face as he talked and fully understood, they both lost their parents and that was something they never planned on.

"Well Ronnie, I reckon things never turn out the way you hope they will. We're proof of that."

They were both silent for a short time. Ronnie noticed a mine along the way. "What is that a mine of some kind?"

"That's what it is, a copper mine."

"It doesn't look very safe, should they be working in there?"

Logan agreed but the miners didn't feel that way.

"They insist they'll be fine but I don't think it looks safe either."

They continued to ride by when some of the men came out of the mine. There was a water barrel and they came out for a drink, it was hot inside the mine so they kept water barrels near by. Just as Ronnie waived to them they heard a noise. Logan stopped the wagon and he and Ronnie ran to help. Logan approached a man to ask how many men were still inside.

"I would say maybe five or six?"

Ronnie couldn't believe he wasn't sure, they should know how many men are working on a job.

"What do you mean maybe, you don't know how many men are working for you?"

The man stopped to think and count the ones who made it out. "Seven out here, six are still in there."

Logan looked at Ronnie.

"Take the wagon back to town and get as many men as possible. Let Noah know what happened."

Ronnie hopped up on the wagon and went as fast as the horses would go, there is no telling if those men are still alive but they had to try. Mean while Logan did what he could with the help of the men who did get out before the mine collapsed. They started digging to get in and start to find the six men inside.

Ronnie made it back to town and went straight to Noah's office.

"Hey Ronnie what's..."

"No time to talk we need men to get out to the copper mine, Logan is there now with seven other men who made it out before it collapsed and there are still six men inside. We need help fast."

Noah acted as quickly as he could, he went outside and called out to any man available to help. Soon most every man was there, Noah explained the situation and men started to head out to the mines. There were women who wanted to be there because their husbands may have been trapped but Noah told them to stay behind until they have more information. Autumn and Cora opened the saloon as a place for the women to gather and wait for news.

Noah, Ronnie and the other men rode out to the mine. Ronnie and Noah filled the wagon with axes, picks and shovels. Noah also grabbed Logan's bag so he could treat the men. Horses and the wagon soon came upon the mine and there were the six men and Logan doing what they could to get through. Logan saw them and Noah held up his medical bag, he jumped off the wagon even before Ronnie stopped it and ran the bag to is brother.

"There isn't a whole lot of progress we made but now all of you are here we can. I won't kid you, this could be dangerous so if that would change your mind you're free to leave. Otherwise let's get busy."

With that being said everyone pitched in, they had lanterns and everything they needed to try and save these men. It wouldn't be long before the sun set so they moved as quickly as possible. Then Noah heard something.

"Hold it everyone, be still for a moment. I heard something."

They all listened carefully, one of the other men heard a sound also. It was a tapping, as if someone in the mine was tapping on something metal.

"I heard it too, come on let's move."

They dug in one area, everyone pitched in the same area when they found an opening. There was a man crying out for help in a very weak voice. Noah and Ronnie climbed through the opening, they found five of the six men nearly unconsciousness. Noah called to Logan to come in with his bag. Ronnie tried to find out from the man who was tapping where the sixth man was.

"Hey, my name is Ronnie."

In a weakened voice the man replied to him.
"I'm Flint Carson, the six man is back there, there's no way he could have made it, his name is Huck Jackson. If he did it would be a damn miracle."

Flint pointed to the area where Huck would be and Noah and Ronnie went to dig their way through while Logan and the others worked to get the rest of the men out. Noah and Ronnie dug and dug when Ronnie hit something.

"Noah, I think I found him."

Noah joined Ronnie and cleared the dirt away to find a mans boot. They knew it had to be him so they kept digging until they could pull him out. Ronnie checked for a pulse but it was too late, this man was dead. Still they pulled his body out so he could have a proper burial.

When they carried him out the men cheered not knowing he was dead. Ronnie held up his hands motioning for the men to stop.

"I'm sorry to say, he didn't make it, he's gone."

Suddenly it was quiet, not a sound from anyone. Noah and Ronnie carried him to the wagon, covered him and took him back to town. The ones who did survive had some scraps and cuts, one had a broken arm. Logan had tended to their needs. Huck Jackson is the husband of Etta Jackson, she ran the hotel in town. Huck Jackson was taken to Logan's office, Noah and Logan went to the hotel to talk to Etta. This is the one thing about his job he hated the most. When they walked into the hotel Etta just stood there, she had a sick feeling in her stomach but knew by the expression on their faces what they had come to tell her.

She broke out in tears and ran to the back room, Noah stayed out front while Logan followed her to the back and do his best to comfort her. Also not an easy task. The couple had just celebrated fifteen years of marriage, they had two children, a boy and a girl.

"Our lives were going so well, now he's gone."

Etta was so hysterical Logan gave her a sedative, he called Noah in the room to have him bring Ronnie to the hotel.

"Maybe Ronnie could run things till we find someone, at least for tonight."

Noah went to find Ronnie, he was at the saloon talking with Autumn when Noah came in and asked Ronnie if he would mind the hotel tonight. Autumn asked about his wife and he told her Logan had to give her a sedative to get through the night. She volunteered to stay with her through the night. Cora and Victoria said they could handle things at the saloon. Word spread like wildfire about Huck Jackson, everyone did what they could for Etta. That night felt particularly unsettling, with good reason. That night was long, seemed like it would never end but Etta was sleeping. The sedative Logan gave her helped but she wasn't resting easy.

When morning came the sun shone through the window waking Etta. At first she didn't remember what happened, then she saw Autumn and in that instant she recalled what happened. Etta began to cry then suddenly thought about their children.

"My God, our children!" Autumn rushed to her side.

"The children are fine, they are with Father Morgan at the church and the other children."

Etta began to wonder how she would tell them about their father. Autumn explained to her that Father Morgan was waiting for her and she and Father would explain things to them together. Etta freshened up as quickly as she could and went to the church with Autumn. Father Morgan saw Autumn and Etta walk in, he took Etta and her children to another room while Autumn stayed with the other children. Sally and Liz were happy to see Autumn, they all sat together while Autumn told them a story. One child raised his hand to ask a question.

"Yes Tommy?"

"Is it true Mr. Jackson died?"

Autumn was stunned, she knew word about his death spread but didn't realize the news would get back to the children.

"Yes Tommy, it is true. Everyone is sad about what happened, I'm sure all of you are too. I know I am."

They all looked at her with sadness on their faces.

"What will happen to his kids?"

"His children still have their mother to take care of them, they can all use your prayers to help them through this. Not just all of you but everyone. Their children may need your help too, being extra nice and doing what you can to help."

Liz raised her hand next.

"Miss Autumn, what can we do to help?"

"Well let me think. How about making a drawing for them and letting them know how sorry you feel for them. You could draw flowers or trees, anything you want. Something to help them through their sadness."

The children all gathered around to think of someway they could help. Tommy raised his hand again.

"Yes Tommy."

"Can we talk about the fun times we all had with Mr. Jackson?"
"Absolutely, that would be very good to help them."

Just then Father Morgan came out with Mrs. Jackson and the children, they were crying as Mrs. Jackson took them by their hands to go home. Father Morgan walked over to talk to the children when Autumn told him she did her best to explain things to them. He thanked her for her help, excusing the children to go to the kitchen there was a snack waiting for them. The children left giving Autumn and Father a chance to talk.

"Noah came to me this morning and told me what happened. Mrs. Jackson will need help with her son and daughter. I told her they are more than welcome to come here with the other children."

"Ronnie just said to me, there is so much happiness he was afraid something bad would happen, he was right unfortunately."

Autumn thanked Father for helping with Huck's family then went back to the saloon where she found Austin waiting for her.

"I came to see how you're doing."

She walked into the kitchen as he followed, she poured some coffee for both of them.

"I went to the church with Etta, Father took her and her children in a room to explain things to them while I stayed with the children, they're pretty good with questions."

"I'm sure you did your best."

"I tried. Things were going so well for a while, now this."

There was a knock on the door, Cora slowly entered and asked if she could come in, Autumn motioned for her to enter.

"Autumn, I realize you hired me to work for you but Mrs. Jackson is going to need help right now and, well I was wondering if you would mind if I took some time off to help Mrs. Jackson at the hotel. She really could..."

"Don't worry, that's fine. I was wondering how she would manage. You're very sweet to help her."

"It's just until she's had some time to take care of things and she feels ready to go back to the hotel. Then I would be back for you."

"Like I said don't worry, that will be fine. If you or she need anything..."

"I promise I'll let you know. Thank you."

Cora left and Autumn took a sigh of relief.

"Well that much is settled. I think I'll make something to take over to them for supper. I'm sure the last thing she feels like doing is cooking."

Austin knew she would find someway to help, that is just Autumn.

"Tell you what, I've been told I make a damn good bar-be-Que chicken, why don't I help you and we can take it over together."

Autumn smiled with approval then Austin went to the general store for some things he would need. While he was gone she started to work on potatoes, green beans and corn bread. She was feeling a little upset in her stomach, she was about to make some tea when she fainted. Too much going on things were getting to her, and with not sleeping well it all affected her. Logan just happen to stop by and find her on the floor. He picked her up and carried her to her room upstairs and lay her on her bed. After a while she started to regain consciousness.

"Honey are you all right? It's me Logan."

She slowly opened her eyes and focused on his face.

"Logan, what happened?"

"You tell me, I came over to check on you and I'm glad I did. You were on the floor, you must have fainted. I think you're working too hard and things are beginning to get to you."

Dabbing her face with the cold cloth she agreed.

"Maybe you're right. I reckon I have been doing a lot lately I just haven't paid much attention to how much."

Austin came back and was looking for Autumn. Logan called downstairs to let him know where she was and how she was doing.

"Well that settles it, I'll take care of supper and you stay here and rest."

"But Austin..."

"No arguments, I can fix supper. Get some sleep, I know you've been having a hard time sleeping."

Logan took note of that and then looked at Autumn.

> "Why didn't you tell me that, not only am I your cousin but I am a doctor. I'm going to my office and I'll be right back, I have just what you need."

Austin fluffed her pillow, covered her with a blanket then kissed her on her forehead.

> "I'll take care of things downstairs while you rest, I'll be be up later to see how you're doing."

When he reached the bottom of the stairs he found Ronnie and Noah waiting to go up to see Autumn. Ronnie was about to climb the stairs until he saw Austin.

> "How is she?"

> "She's fine and resting comfortably. Autumn has been pushing herself with the fair, cooking for all the men rebuilding the orphanage and now wanting to help Mrs. Jackson. I'm not saying she shouldn't be doing all of this but she has been working really hard and not taking much time for herself."

Noah had noticed that also.

> "She has seemed a little tired lately."

Austin mentioned her sleeping habits.

> "She told me she has difficulty sleeping, Logan went to his office to get something to help her sleep."

Logan walked in on the conversation.

> "I have it right here, make sure she takes two of these if she starts having difficulty sleeping."

Ronnie never heard this before.

> "She's having difficulty sleeping?"

Austin didn't realize he wasn't aware of this.

"I'm sorry, I thought she told you. Several times a week she has a hard time sleeping, nightmares keep her awake." Ronnie looked at Noah and Logan.

"I knew everything that happened in Cheyenne was bothering her but she never told me about the nightmares."

"She probably didn't want to worry you knowing her like I do. As far back as Noah and I can remember she's been that way. Well these pills should help her sleep I'm sure."

Autumn was so exhausted she slept the rest of that day and through the night. This was the first night she was able to sleep peacefully. When she did wake up she realized it was morning. She rushed downstairs to the kitchen and found Austin cooking.

"What happened? How did I manage to sleep so long?"

"Logan gave you something to help you sleep. You slept just about through breakfast."

"I did want to take supper over to Mrs. Jackson."

"I finished that and took it over. She said she would come over to thank you later after lunch."

Autumn thanked him for all his help and decided she was going to take a long hot bath then she would be down to help with lunch. Ronnie stopped in to check on her, she went over to give him a hug, then he wanted to know why she didn't tell him about her nightmares.

"It's nothing really, besides you have your own problems."

"I don't want to hear that, we're family and don't forget that. We have each other and Logan and Noah and we stick together no matter what understand?"

"Let me ask you a question, do always tell me your problems?" "Uh... no but that's different."

"Oh really! How? I don't want to hear cause I'm a man."

"Did you say breakfast is ready?"

"I thought so, I'll let Austin know you're here. Austin cooked, he can cook up a storm. I'll let him know you're here, I'm going up for a bath. Talk to you later, love you."

She hugged him once more then went to the kitchen to let Austin know he was at a table, then she went upstairs. A few minutes later Austin brought out a plate and some coffee for Ronnie.

"So Austin, did she sleep last night?"

"She slept, from the time you and Noah stopped over till this morning. I knew she was tired, but this morning she seems better than I've seen her."

"I hope so. Thanks for breakfast." "That's okay, enjoy."

Austin went back to the kitchen to clean up then he had things to get done. He stayed long enough for Autumn to come back down and take over, then he told her he would see her later.

"I must say you do look especially beautiful this morning." Autumn looked at him and he knew what she was thinking.

"Okay I'm sorry, but you're my sister and I love you."

"I love you too but we have our own lives and we're grown. That doesn't mean I don't love you or want you out of my life but if I ever do need help I will come to you."

Ronnie had a lost look on his face.

"It's just...you are my kid sister and I am responsible for you."

"Wrong, you're responsible for you. I may be your kid sister but that doesn't make you responsible for me. We're grown adults and you will always be my brother no matter what."

Ronnie shook his head, he knew deep down she was right.

"Well then with that said I better head back and I will see you later Miss Snyder."

"Very well Mr. Snyder."

Autumn went to see Etta Jackson to see if there is anything she could do for her. One look at her and you could tell she didn't sleep all night, how difficult it would be to lose your husband and be left with the two children you're so use to raising with him. What will things be like now that he's gone?

> "I brought over some muffins Austin made fresh this morning. I thought maybe you and the kids might be hungry. Let me put on some coffee."

> "Oh please I don't want to put you to any trouble."

> "It's no trouble really. I'll be right back."

Autumn put on the coffee then found a plate for the muffins. Her daughter, Nora, walked in and saw Autumn in the kitchen.

> "Who are you?"

She turned to find the little girl standing and staring at her.

> "Hi, I'm Autumn, what's your name?"

> "My name is Nora. I don't have a daddy anymore."

Autumn fought hard to not let tears fall, she had a huge lump in throat that made it hard to swallow. She turned her head to clear her eyes then went back to the little girl.

> "Nora, that's such a pretty name for a pretty girl. I'm sorry about your daddy sweetheart. You know what? I brought muffins, would you like one?"

Nora looked at the muffins then up at Autumn.

> "Go on, they're very good."

Nora took a muffin and took a bite. A small smile on he face told Autumn they were very good.

> "How about some milk to go with that muffin?"

Nora nodded and sat at the table while Autumn poured her some milk. Then her brother, Cooper, walked in and saw the muffin she was eating.

> "Hi, my name is Cooper. May I have a muffin and some milk too please?"

Autumn motioned for him to come and sit at the table, she gave him a glass of milk and a muffin. She watched as they enjoyed breakfast. By now the coffee was ready and she poured two cups and set up a tray with some muffins and took them in to Etta. She sat down next to her placing the tray on the coffee table.

"The children are having milk and a muffin, I hope that's all right?"

"Yes, thank you so much. I look around and I see Huck everywhere, only he's not really here. Oh why did this have to happen?"

Etta began crying and Autumn put her arm around her to comfort her. Then she thought about her parents. Why do these things have to happen? None of this seems fair, but what is? Etta would not be alone, everyone in town will be there for her.

"We're burying him tomorrow."

"Is there anything at all I can do?"

"Not that I can think of, all the preparations have been made but thank you so much for your offer, I appreciate that."

"That's what we're here for, I'll be bringing dinner by for you and the kids later."

"That's really sweet but not necessary."

"Don't worry, you need time for you and the children right now. I'll stop by later."

Etta thanked her and walked her to the door. That day seemed so long for Etta. The men held off building out of respect to Etta and the kids, it was a solemn day. You could feel the unhappiness in the air. Ronnie was working on his ranch just to work off energy and anger about the copper mine. Things in town were slow and people stopped by to see Etta and the kids and pay respects. Autumn stopped at the hotel to see how Cora was doing. She walked in and Cora was just standing there trying to look busy.

"Hey, how is everything here?"

"Not well, no one has come into town so things are slow here. I wish there could be some kind of business, Etta is going to need the money."

"Don't worry, things will look up soon I'm sure."

113

Just then twelve men came in to register, Cora was so happy. They really didn't need the room but they did it to help Etta knowing she would need the money. They all worked with Huck in the mine and were good friends with him. This was their way of helping his family now. Cora and Autumn were so pleased at their generosity.

"I'll see you later Cora, I'm taking supper over to the Jackson house later, I'll bring you something too."

"Thank you so much."

Autumn stopped in to see Logan at his office, he was tending to his patients. It was a slow day for him also, not too many needed tending to.

"Hey Autumn, not very busy and those who have come in is asking about Etta and her family."

"I was just over to see them, I dropped off some muffins for them. It's sad over there, I wish I could do more."

"Time Autumn, they'll make through. They're stronger than even they realize. Just like you and Ronnie."

She had to stop and think for a moment then realized he's right. "Well I have to get back, stop over for supper later."

Logan shook his head as a patient walked in, they went back to the examination room. Her next stop was Noah's office, she found him sitting there working on papers.

"Hey Autumn, what brings you by? Everything okay?"

"As well as can be expected, I just wanted to stop by and invite you over to the saloon for supper, Ronnie and Logan will be stopping in so you three can sit down for a talk. It will be good to see the three of you together."

"I'll be there, thank you."

When she left the jailhouse she happened to look over at the graveyard, men were digging a spot for Mr. Jackson. Then after a minute she went to the church walked in and sat in a pew in front. Autumn got down on her knees to pray for the family. Tears started streaming down her face, she looked up but couldn't stop crying. Autumn ran out of the church and down the street, she just kept running. Noah happened to look out his window and saw her, he left to go after her.

Autumn ran past the stores in town and just kept going until she fell. That was when Noah caught up with her, he grabbed hold of her and all she could do was beat her fists on him and scream, she was so full of anger she couldn't help herself. One of the women came out of the general store and saw them, she rushed to Logan's office to tell him what was happening. He grabbed his bag and went out to them but Autumn was fighting and struggling.

"Hold her down Noah I need to give her a sedative."

Noah did the best he could even while she was still screaming. Once the sedative took affect Noah carried her back to the saloon and up to her room.

"Logan, she's struggling with their parents death and Huck Jackson is just a reminder of that. Something is happening with her."

"I know, this is a mild sedative so she won't sleep as long as the last time. Maybe we can talk to her and figure out what's going on in her mind. Till then can you take a ride out to let Ronnie know what happened? Maybe he could help us figure out what to do for her."

"I'm on my way."

Logan went back to his office while Austin sat with her, and Noah rode out to see Ronnie and tell him what happened. He wasn't happy hearing about this. "Noah I don't know what I'm going to do, I'm worried."

"Logan gave her a mild sedative so she won't sleep as long as last time. Maybe we can all sit down and try to talk to her."

Ronnie said he would get cleaned up and come into town, hopefully between the three of them they can figure this out. Noah went back to town and talked to Logan and let him know Ronnie will be in town shortly and they could all get together to help her somehow. Sally happened to see Autumn running out of the church, she walked over to Logan's office to see if she was all right. Sally walked in quietly, when Logan came out of the other room he saw her standing there with the saddest look on her face.

"Doctor Logan sir, is Miss Autumn okay? I saw her running out of the church crying."

Logan realized then Autumn probably didn't even see Sally.

"Come here sweetheart, sit on my lap. Now first does Father Morgan know you're here?"

"No sir, I was worried about Miss Autumn."

"I understand that, but when he finds out you're not there don't you think he'll be worried about you the way you are about Miss Autumn?"

She hung her head down almost in tears.

"I didn't think of that, I don't want him to worry. I was just scared for Miss Autumn."

Sally began crying, she became scared thinking she would be in trouble. Logan picked her up and hugged her.

"Now now it's all right. I'll take you back and talk to Father, but the next time you come over to visit you have to tell him. Okay?"

"I will, I promise."

"Now Miss Autumn. She is sad because not long ago she lost her mom and dad."

"Does that mean she's as orphan like me?"

Logan couldn't help but giggle.

"Not exactly honey, she's a big girl, but I suppose in a way she is an orphan. Only she has her brother, Mr. Ronnie, and me and Noah. We're still a family. Now, what do you say I walk you back to the church. Before we go would you like a licorice whip?"

Sally had a smile on her face.

"Oh yes please, and may I please have one for Liz? She is my friend."

"Tell you what, I have a big bag full of licorice, let's take it over and you can share it with all the kids, how does that sound?"

"Thank you Mr. Logan, thank you so much."

Logan took Sally's hand and together they walked to the church. When they went inside Father Morgan looked at Sally.

"Sally, where have you been and why did you take off without telling me?"

Sally knew she was in trouble but Logan spoke up to defend her if possible.

> "Father, Sally came over to my office, she was worried about my cousin Autumn. She had ran out crying, our guess is she didn't see Sally."

Father Morgan's face changed.

> "Sally would you mind going downstairs to play with the other children? I would like to talk to Mr. Logan privately."

> "Yes Father, and thank you Mr. Logan. I'll share this with the other kids."

> "You're welcome Sally, go on and play. I'll see you later."

Sally went downstairs to play while Logan explained the situation with Father Morgan.

> "I see, I'm so sorry. I didn't even know she was here. I'll forgive Sally of punishment this time. I know how close she is to Autumn. My prayers are with you and her. If there is anything I can do to help…"

> "I will let you know, thank you."

Logan turned and walked out the door, he still had patients coming in later and Ronnie may be at his office by now. When he was closer to his office he recognized the wagon as Ronnie's. He rushed over and inside where he found Noah and Ronnie talking.

> "How is she?"

> "That's a good question. It were as if she didn't even know Noah or me. I gave her a mild sedative so soon she should be waking up."

> "Does anyone know what happened?"

> "No, Sally saw her crying and then run out the door. I just walked her back to the church. I'm guessing Autumn didn't see her. When I left Austin was sitting with her." Ronnie sat on the desk rubbing his head.

> "I don't know what to do for her, I don't know what's wrong?"

The three of them sat there talking trying to figure out what they can do for her. All they could come up with is to question her about what happened. Logan's next patient wasn't due in for about another hour so they went to check on Autumn and try to find out what was wrong.

117

They walked over to the saloon where Cora was taking care of customers, when she looked up and saw them come in she went over to them concerned for Autumn.

"Austin is still up there with her, I think was waking up just a few minutes ago."

Ronnie thanked her then they went upstairs to talk with her. They knocked, Austin opened the door. When he saw who it was he told them he would give them privacy with her.

"She's calm right now, what ever happened. I'm not so sure she remembers."

Then he went downstairs, Ronnie rushed over to her and sat next beside her.

"So Autumn, what happened?"

The look on her face was clueless, as if she didn't know what they were talking about.

"What do you mean what happened? About what? I over slept and should have been up a long time ago, I wanted to go see Mrs. Jackson."

They all looked at each other, it were as if she lost her memory. Noah looked at her and took her hand.

"Sweetheart you did go over there this morning, then you went to the church."

The gazing look on her face told them she didn't remember. Logan stepped over and sat next to her, he was checking her head for injury. Not one bump was on her head.

"Oh yes, I do remember going there now, but how did I end up here? I wanted to go to the church to pray for her and her kids."

Logan, Noah and Ronnie looked at each other, then Logan looked at Autumn.

"Honey we're going to let you rest, if you need anything call us. We'll be here for you."

She was confused and didn't understand what any of them were talking about, but she was tired and drifted off to sleep. The boys left her room and went downstairs. Ronnie was very concerned.

"Logan, what is happening to her?"

"The best I can say is she's suppressing something. Whatever it is she'll remember when her mind tells her it's time. I really don't think there's anything we can do until then."

Logan didn't like saying it any more than Ronnie liked hearing it but there was nothing more that could be done. Austin over heard everything they talked about.

"So there's not one thing we can do to help her?"

Logan nodded and was no happier about it than anyone else.

"I'm afraid not. Look she's my cousin and if there were something don't you think I would do it?"

They all looked at him, no one has ever seen him like this before.

"I'm sorry, it's eating me up inside that I can't do anything. I'm a doctor damn it, I trained to heal people and there isn't one thing I can do for her."

With that Logan left slamming the door on the way out. Ronnie and Austin both looked at Noah.

"He hates these cases. Logan feels as though he fails as a doctor if he can't heal them and he knows better. He just doesn't like to be beat, and that is how he feels right now. Don't take anything he said personally, he's a sore loser when it comes to healing."

Ronnie went back to his ranch, Noah went back to the jailhouse and Austin went for a ride. Autumn slept the rest of that day and through the night. When she woke the next morning it were as though yesterday never happened. She as well as many of the towns people attended the funeral for Huck Jackson. The sun was shining but still it was a gloomy day. Father Morgan gave a wonderful eulogy. The men that Huck worked with all expressed they condolences to his family. When it was over everyone went back home, Autumn and Cora walked Etta and the children home to make sure they were safe.

"Thank you both for walking us home, please don't think I'm being cruel but we would like to be left alone today. We will manage, thank you and everyone for your thoughtfulness."

With that she closed the door, Autumn and Cora went home. Cora looked at Autumn.

"Well thank you, she'll come around she just needs some time." "I know, I'll see you tomorrow. Good night."

Chapter 5

It's been two weeks since the funeral, Victoria and Tim are back from their vacation and was sad to hear about Huck Jackson and the mines. Things are beginning to move along and Etta is slowly getting her life together. Plans for the fair are back in motion and the building for the orphanage is coming along fine. Etta made a point of going to the saloon to see Autumn and Cora.

"Miss Snyder, I would like to donate this to the auction for the fair you're planning. Some of these things belonged to Huck and I know he would want them to be used for good purposes. I can't keep them, I won't have the room any longer."

"Why? Is something wrong?"

"No, nothing like that. Now the house is too big for just the kids and me so I'm selling it and buying a smaller place. I actually all ready sold and I'll be signing papers for the our new place, and it's closer to town so it all works out."

Autumn looked at her face, she will still need more time but she is working through things.

"Are you sure you want to give these things up?"

"I'm sure, I'm keeping certain things of course, but Huck would want these to go to good use. He use to talk about how he wanted to do something for the kids but we didn't have extra money and he didn't have the time to help build. Not with his time working in the mines. Please take this as our donation, this is what you can do for me."

Etta really reached her heart and again offered to help if there was any way she could. Victoria walked in and saw Etta, she went over to offer her condolences and hugged her. Etta was getting stronger each passing day.

"Etta, Tim and I were wondering if you and the children could come to our home for supper tonight? We would love to have you and the children. Also if you wouldn't mind, maybe give a new bride some hints. I've never been married before and I'm still learning, if I wouldn't be troubling you."

"No trouble, we would love to be there, would six be all right?"
"That's perfect, we can't wait to see all of you."

Etta thanked her and Autumn then went on her way. Autumn cleared her throat and stared at Victoria.

"Is something wrong?"

"You need help being a bride?I happen to know from Tim you do a remarkable job taking care of him and the house."

Victoria went to the kitchen to pour some coffee for her and Autumn.

"She doesn't have to know that. If I told her the truth do you think she would come over?"

Again Autumn stared at her.

"No, you're right she probably wouldn't. You are very good."

They laughed and went to the storage room to sort through everything that was donated. Autumn told Victoria everything that was going on about the fair and Ronnie had things ready at his ranch to hold it there.

"That sounds marvelous, I really think this is going to be a great success. Look at all these things, I'm sure you will raise more than enough money for the orphanage."

"I hope so, if there is extra it can be used for food or anything else they may need."

They were both starting to get excited about this fair.

"Autumn, Tim wanted me to tell you if you need an auctioneer he has done that before, he would be more than happy to volunteer to help."

"That would be great, consider him hired, and thank him so much for me. Things are really falling into place."

They sorted things into boxes and packed them to take to the ranch. Cora came into the saloon as Autumn and Victoria were carrying boxes out to the wagon.

"Autumn, I really need to talk to you please."

"Of course, is something wrong?"

"No nothing is wrong, but my girlfriend is having a baby and her husband is out of town and can't get back in time. I'm so much closer than her husband is and she wants me to help her. Would you mind terribly if I left town about a week?"

How could anyone refuse that.

"Go and be safe. Good luck to you and your friend. We'll see you when you get back."

"Thank you so much. I took care of all the books so everything will be good till I get back so no worries there."

Autumn trusted her, she has never let her down yet. Victoria and Autumn were leaving to pack up the wagon as an Indian was walking through the door. The women stared not knowing if they should be frightened or not.

"Please do not be frightened. My name is Arjun, I know your brother Ronnie. He saved my sister. I would like to see him, can you tell how to reach him, please?"

The women felt safe knowing that he is a friend.

"Yes I can. We are headed out to his ranch shortly if you would like to follow us. As soon as we finish loading the wagon we will be on our way."

Arjun looked around. He helped the women load the wagon and soon they were on their way to the ranch. Autumn had no idea why this Indian was looking for Ronnie, but he seemed harmless enough. Surely there was something Ronnie never mentioned about his trip to Anaconda. The ranch was just up ahead, Ronnie must have been inside, he was not in site. Autumn hopped down from the wagon.

"I'll see if he's inside."

She went to the door and knocked calling his name. When he came out he was surprised to see Arjun.

"Welcome my friend, it's so good to see you again. Is anything wrong?"

Arjun dismounted his horse and walked over to Ronnie.

"Nothing wrong, I was here about a week ago to see you and heard about the fire and the orphanage. You did a great service to my sister, we would like to return the favor. Several of my people are ready to come and help rebuild. Our father insists."

The women were astounded, they couldn't believe what they heard.

"My friend we will gladly welcome you and your people. Thank you."
"They are not far, we set up camp close by, I will go and bring them."

Arjun nodded to the women then was on his way.

"Ronnie, is there anything you would like to tell me?"

"In short his sister was being attacked, I stopped to help her. If I hadn't come along when I did there is no telling what that man would have done to her. Her people are grateful, that's all."

"That's all he says, that is a big deal. You saved a woman's life and you never said a word? I can't believe you."

Ronnie looked at her and shook his head.

"I'm sure that's not the reason you came out here. What's up?"

"We brought the donations out for the auction, my storage room will not hold anymore. Is it all right to store them in your barn?" He smiled.

"Of course, let me help you."

It was easier with Ronnie helping, he carried the heavier boxes. They were very appreciative for his help, they took longer to load than unload.

"Well I hate to run but I do have to get back, I'll see you later. Thanks Ronnie."

Things were going so well no one wanted to talk about anything negative thinking it may bring more bad luck. This town has had more than it's share all ready in the short amount of time Autumn and Ronnie lived here. When they arrived back in town they saw Cora waiting

123

for the train so they stopped over to wish her well. They hugged each other and hoped that Cora would have a safe trip.

> We'll see you when you get back, we wish your friend well and a healthy baby."

> "Thank you both, I'll see you when I get back."

The train was pulling in and they waved goodbye.

> "A baby, something happy for a change, maybe that will break the luck we've been having."

Victoria looked at Autumn.

> "Well what about what Ronnie did? He's lucky, he could have been killed."

> "I can't believe Ronnie never said a word about what happened, you're so right he could have been killed. Arjun didn't have to come here but it was very nice of him to bring some of his people to help."

The fair would take place in about a week so the women had to get busy and pull things together. Donations, prizes and lists of baked and canned goods were pouring in, this was sure to be a success. Now it was just a matter of organization. Victoria's husband, Tim walked in the saloon to talk to Autumn and his wife.

> "Hey Autumn, Victoria. Remember when I went to help my mother in. In Idaho? Well we talked about the orphanage and the children. Anyway my mother has always had a place in her heart for children, so I just received this money today. It's a donation for the children."

He handed the envelope to Autumn, when she opened it there was one hundred dollars inside.

> "Tim this is a lot of money. I can't take your mother's money from her but it is a very generous gesture."

> "Don't worry about my mother, she has plenty of money. She would feel hurt if you didn't take it, please."

Autumn didn't want to hurt or insult anyone, so she graciously accepted the money.

"Please thank her for us, let her know how much we appreciate this money and assure her it will go to good use."

Tim promised he would tell her. Autumn asked him to please sit down with his wife Victoria, and she would bring them out some lunch. Tim made her promise she would have lunch with them. Victoria went to the kitchen with Autumn to help her.

"Victoria you're a lucky lady, your Tim is a very special man."

"I know, I don't know how I got to be so lucky, but I am grateful."

The three of them sat down for lunch and go over the details about the fair, it would be coming up soon. The building was coming along even with the setbacks they had, the rain and the funeral. They built about a forth of the building and it was looking great, including the additional room they decided to add on for the children. Autumn was excited about all of this, and the towns people were really giving their all to help.

Ronnie had stopped in the saloon and saw Tim Victoria and Autumn sitting at the table. He walked over to order lunch for himself, he's been so busy working on things at the ranch to get ready for the fair.

"Wait till you see how I fixed up the barn, it's ready for the auction, and I have a surprise for you Autumn. I built a dunking booth, I thought you could raise more money that way and it would fun."

"You did that? This is going to be a great fair and a lot of fun. How can I thank you?"

"A free lunch sounds good to me."

"You earned it, be right back."

Noah and Logan came in for lunch and they were asking about the fair. It's what everyone is talking about. The people could use something like this. Autumn brought everyone lunch and when she looked up she couldn't believe who walked through the door.

"Marsha, how wonderful it is to see you, but why are you here?" Marsha smiled and hugged Autumn.

"My mother passed away two weeks ago, it's over. I'll be staying at her home in Texas."

Autumn was so glad to see her but sorry to hear about her mother, even though they both knew what the outcome would be it wasn't any easier.

"I'm really very sorry Marsha."

"She went peacefully, in her sleep and she didn't suffer. Anyway it's time to move on. I got wind of the fair you're planning to raise money. I wanted to be here for that. After all a piece of me still lives here. It was awful what happened but you're doing a wonderful thing. I want want to help you anyway I can."

This was going to be a wonderful time, Autumn wished Marsha could stay in Anaconda but she understood Marsha's situation. She was telling Marsha about the dunk tank Ronnie made for the fair, how he saved a woman's life, Etta's husband, getting her all caught up on what was happening. It were as if Marsha never left, she felt at home again and it felt great.

A week had gone by and everything was set for the fair. The auction, dunking tank, pony rides, games and clowns and more. Booths were set up and ready to go, the children at the church were excited and couldn't wait to go to the fair the next day.

"Well sis, I wish you the best outcome for this fair. Mom and Dad would be so proud of you."

"Thank you Ronnie. I appreciate that. I'm hoping for the best. Well I better get going, tomorrow is the big day. Good night, thank your so much again for everything."

Autumn gave her brother a hug then rode back into town. Ronnie stood there waving till she was out of site, then he turned in for the night. The night was a little cooler, the day was really hot it and the breeze felt good gently blowing through the opened window. Ronnie slept comfortably that night and when he was waken by the rooster, he was feeling exceptionally well. Autumn, Tim, Victoria, Marsha and Etta all came out together to get ready for the fair. They brought muffins for breakfast and Ronnie made coffee.

"I think everything looks better today for some reason. I don't know why!"

"I think it's your imagination, you're just excited."

She was excited, they all pitched in to get ready, the pony's were brought in, the people working the booths arrived and everyone was setting up. Father Morgan arrived with the children, they were anxious to come to the fair. Soon and hopefully others will be arriving. Farmers were bringing in their crops to sell, the clowns arrived and they were blowing up balloons for the kids. Once everyone was there Autumn wanted to make a small speech. She stood on the platform Ronnie built and asked for everyone's attention.

> "Hello everyone, I want to thank all of you in advance for your help, whether it was donation, volunteering to work a booth, building the the booths rebuilding the orphanage, whatever part you played in I can't thank you enough. This fair is for a good cause, the children. I hope this will be a success and please, I hope everyone enjoys themselves. Thank you."

Father Morgan offered a prayer before the festivities began, they bowed their heads while he prayed then everyone said Amen. The people clapped and were raring to begin. Marsha noticed a wagon full of people coming.

> "Look, People are starting to come. Let's get started."

Noah and Logan brought people in by wagon and would take them back when they were ready. People shopping around and the kids playing games. What a beautiful site it was and to hear the laughter, see the children riding pony's and playing games. Soon the ranch was full of people. There must have been people from surrounding towns coming to the fair, people no one knew were there having a great time.

The auction was about to begin, the barn was so full people were standing. The baked and canned goods were selling so quickly, the clowns were entertaining the children. Everyone needed a break and this was it, relaxing and enjoying themselves. Ronnie, Noah and Logan took turns in the dunking tank and riding people back and forth. This fair was very successful, Autumn was so pleased.

The day seemed to fly by and now people were going home, there was a slight chill in the air and the breeze blowing. There wasn't one thing left, everything sold. Noah took the money box and accompanied Autumn home with it making sure she would be safe. Noah glanced over at Autumn, she looked as though she could fall asleep at any time.

> "Autumn...you're tired. You should be you worked so hard on this."

> "I think I'm ready for bed, I may even sleep in tomorrow."

> "Why don't you close the saloon for one day, it won't hurt you."

That did sound nice and she could use the rest.

> "Maybe I will. Why not?"

He pulled the wagon in front of the saloon and walked her to her room making sure she is safe.

> "Thank you for bringing me home. I haven't seen Austin much this entire time."

Noah smiled at her, he knew deep down she cared for him.

> "You're not the only one who worked hard, he's been doing anything he could help with to make this work. He knows how much this means to you."

Then he kissed her on the cheek and said good night. Autumn closed her door locked it then put the money in the safe. She walked over to the window gazing in the sky. Austin really is special, but she wasn't sure she was ready for a relationship just now. No matter how much she enjoyed his company and spending time with him. She was feeling confused, for now all she really wanted was to sleep.

The next morning Autumn was up early to take the money to Father Morgan, when she arrived at the church he wasn't there, but Noah was.

> "Morning Noah, where is Father Morgan?"

He pulled her aside and asked Etta to keep an eye on the kids.

> "We need to talk, let's go to the jailhouse."

Autumn didn't know what to think, she was starting to worry.

> "What's going on? Where is Father Morgan?" "That's what we need to talk about?"

> "Oh no, is something wrong?"

> "Calm down, let me explain. Father Morgan wasn't living here very long in Anaconda. Being a priest no one ever thought to question his identity. Late last night a sheriff from Blackwell Texas came looking for him."

Autumn had an ill feeling in her stomach.

> "I'm feeling nauseous."

"He goes from town to town posing as priests, doctors, anything. He tricked people into giving him money and as soon as anyone became suspicious he would move on to another town. I'm sorry sweetie."

She sat in the chair with such disbelief, it just couldn't be real. "What about the money I had given to him all ready"

"You were lucky, when the sheriff and I went to get him, we found the money he had in a bag he was packing. Here it is, you may want to keep it in your safe."

Noah handed her the money and she put it in her bag with the money that was raised at the fair. Logan walked in and saw her sitting in the chair. That look on her face said it all.

"Autumn, are you all right?"

Noah shook his head feeling bad for her, she trusted him.

"Noah I'll take her home, she's in a state and shouldn't be alone."
"Thanks, let me know how she is okay?"

Logan agreed then took Autumn by her arm and walked her to the saloon.

"I have to put this away, I'll be back down."

"I'll get us some coffee."

Victoria came out from the kitchen and saw Logan, he told her what happened and like Autumn she was stunned.

"I'll bring out some coffee, would you like some breakfast? I just made hot cakes."

"That sounds great, I am hankering for something, thank you." Autumn came back downstairs and sat at the table with Logan.

"Coffee is always good in the morning for some reason, not that it isn't any other time."

Logan knew she was upset.

"Victoria said she made some hot cakes, maybe you should have some."

"I don't know, I'm not so hungry right now."

"Autumn, look at it this way. You got back the money you gave him and still have the money you were about to give him. That's good, it could have all been gone with him but he was caught before he could get away with it, that's something."

She looked at Logan and smiled a bit.

"You're right, then these kids would have nothing."

Victoria came out with the coffee and hot cakes for Logan, Autumn asked her to bring a small stack for her. Suddenly she was hungry. Then she had a thought.

"Logan, what about the kids what will happen to them?"

"Etta will be staying at the church with the kids until we can find someone to take over. She said this was something she needed for her. Don't worry."

Autumn felt better knowing the children would be in good hands. After she and Logan finished breakfast he went to his office to get his bag. He wanted to examine the children and make sure they're healthy. He always examined them and never charged anyone, they're kids and they need medical attention.

Things were beginning to get back to normal, soon the orphanage would be rebuilt and completely running smoothly once more. The men were making better progress than before with the help of the Blackfoot Indians. The town was in disbelief about Father Morgan, now they would need a new priest but they would be very careful about who would take over that position.

Austin walked in the saloon to see Autumn, Victoria went to the kitchen to let her know he was looking for her.

"Hey Austin, how are you?"

"I'm good but I did want to check on you."

"Me! Why?"

She seemed surprised as if he expected something to be wrong.

"I heard about Father Morgan and I knew you would be worried."

"That, yes well. Etta is taking care of the children and Noah was able to get back the money I gave him so far, but he did cheat this town. What a shame Noah couldn't get back their money."

Austin agreed, then he moved on to talk to her about going out that evening.

"I would really enjoy your company tonight, how does supper and a ride down by the lake sound?"

"That sounds wonderful, peaceful and quiet. What time should I be ready?"

"How does six sound?" "Perfect, I'll be ready."

Austin kissed her on the cheek and promised to see her later. As he was leaving Marsha walked in the door.

"Marsha, good morning. Would you like some coffee?"

"I would love some thank you. The place looks great, I knew you would be great here. How are things with you?"

Autumn poured the coffee then sat down for a spell.

"Things are great. I love the town, the people, everything about Anaconda."

Marsha looked at her that said, you know what I mean.

"Okay, I'm still working on certain but even they are getting easier to deal with.

"Yes I do, and that's good also."

"How about you? Do you think you might come back?"

Marsha was in thought, she really did enjoy being a part of this place.

"I don't think so, I have a new life now, but this is a great excuse for a trip to visit."

Autumn was hoping she would come back.

"I have my mother's place to take care of, and..."

"And what?"

"To be honest, I met someone. I never gave a relationship a thought, but he really struck me. We get along great, we see each other often. He's an unexpected pleasure."

"That sounds wonderful, I'm happy for you."

"I'm staying here for a few more days then I'll be leaving. I just needed a break from...things."

Autumn knew what she meant. Somethings just are too difficult and you have to do what you need to to deal with them. However that may be.

"So how are you and that young man that I saw leaving doing?"

"We're fine, he's really great with the kids, very thoughtful and gallant."

"How serious are you about him?" "Marsha!"

"Come on, I can tell he's really smitten with you."

She began to blush a little, she does like him.

"We haven't been courting very long, but I do care for him."

Marsha looked in her eyes.

"You more than care for him, you have that look."

"Maybe so much had been happening in town we haven't had much time to spend together. We'll see, in time."

Then Autumn stood up and went to get Marsha some of Victoria's muffins. Everyone loved them and couldn't get enough. Autumn came back with a bag full of them to give to Marsha.

"These muffins is a real crowed pleaser, Victoria is famous for them."

"Thank you, I'm sure I'll enjoy them. I have some visiting and some shopping to do. I'll see you soon."

The day went on and everything was going as usual, the women going to the dress shop, the general store was busy, even the hotel was busy. The train was in, the whistle was blowing and the passengers getting off. Cora was one of those passengers, she couldn't wait to go to the saloon and see Autumn and Victoria. She walked in and set down her bags as Victoria came out of the kitchen.

"Autumn, come quick, Cora is back!"

They ran over to hug her and welcome her home. Autumn took a step back to look her over.

"Don't misunderstand but I thought you would be gone another couple of days at least!"

"That was the original plan but she had her baby early and her sister just happened to come for a visit. She said she knew my friend, Ada,was due to have the baby and that her husband would be out of town so she came to stay with her. She'll take care of Ada and the baby until her husband comes home. So here I am!"

Cora said she wanted to take her things upstairs then she would come back to help Autumn and Victoria. This day was going so well no one wanted it to end. Ronnie was at his ranch working around the house making repairs that were needed. The fence around the barn was repaired, he really would like to buy more horses, maybe a few head of cattle. Right now the money he has will cover the repairs on the house.

Ronnie rode into to town to help on with building for a while then he would stop at the general store to pick up some things he needed for the repairs. When he reached the building Arjun was there with five of his people. Things were looking really great and coming along fine. Ronnie hopped off the wagon, talked to Arjun a minute or two then they went back to work. As they worked Arjun asked Ronnie how things are going with him, Ronnie explained how he bought a ranch and the repairs needed. Now he would like to buy some horses and cattle.

"Ronnie, there is a rodeo in West Yellowstone, not very far from here. The winnings is two thousand dollars. That could help you."

He has Ronnie's attention.

"Really, that sounds great. I'll have to sign up, do you know how long I have to sign up for this?"

"By the end of this week. I'm sure you have a very good chance. You should go."

"I can't leave you and everyone behind, you're here because of me. It wouldn't be right to leave you and your friends."

"Friends help each other, I'm here to help because you helped my people. Go, you need to enter. We'll be fine."

Ronnie was tempted, it would be great if he did win, a big help.

"You convinced me, we may not be blood brothers, but I do consider you to be a brother. You know if there is anything I can do for you or your people, please see me."

"Yes I know. Now go."

Ronnie smiled and thanked him again. He stopped in to see Autumn, Logan and Noah before he left. Autumn packed him some food and wished him well. "Be safe Ronnie."

"Don't worry I'll be fine. See you when I get back."

Tim walked in just before Ronnie left.

"Hey Ronnie, looks like your headed out?"

"Hey Tim, I am. I'm going to sign up for a rodeo in West Yellowstone. The winnings is two thousand dollars, if I can win that money it sure would help me to get a start on my ranch."

"That would be great, they have the highest paid winnings of any rodeo around. Good luck."

"Thank you, see you when I get back."

Tim looked around for Victoria. Autumn looked at him with a smile.

"Have a seat, I'll have Victoria bring you some food and coffee."
"Thanks."

Tim sat waiting patiently to see his bride. When she came out of the kitchen she had his coffee and a plate of food.

"Hi, what brings you here?"

"I just wanted to see my wife. Do you have a moment to sit with me?"
"Sure, is something wrong?"

"No nothing. I'm going to go help with the new building. There isn't much to do around the ranch today and those kids are very important. I received a telegram today, not long ago."

"Really? Is it important?"

"You can say that. My cousin Jake just bought a larger ranch, sold his smaller one. Things are going very well for him. He asked me about buying the ranch he's in right now. I don't think I want to leave here, this place is home to me. How do you feel about this?"

Victoria looked at him just wondering.

"Are you sure you wouldn't want to buy his ranch?"

Tim just stared at her wondering why she would ask that, especially when she seemed so happy here.

"Do you want me to? You seem so happy here."

"It's just if you really want to buy his ranch I think you should. We can be happy anywhere, I am happy here but I'm thinking of you."

"I'm sure. I don't want to live anywhere else. I'd better get going if I'm going to help them build. I'll see you home for supper."

"Be careful, I'll see you then."

Autumn watched the two of them from the kitchen, they seemed so happy together. She saw Austin walk in as Tim was leaving and she went out to see him.

"Autumn, how are things here?"

"Things are very well thank you. How are you."

"I'm well also. I know your brother went out of town but there is a man who brought in a horse. A beauty too, anyway he was supposed to sell it to someone who changed their mind. This guy wanted to get rid of the horse because he can't afford to keep it anymore. He wants this horse to have a good home so I thought about Ronnie. Do you think he would be interested?"

Autumn thought this is something she can do for him, he was always doing for her.

"How much is he asking?"

"He only wants one hundred, practically giving it away."

"I'll be right back."

She went upstairs as fast as she could, went to her savings can for the money. Then back downstairs as fast as lightening.

"Here is the money, it'll be my present to Ronnie. Would you mind buying the horse for me and later we can take him to the ranch. I want to surprise him."

Austin did as she asked him to and told her he'll see her at six. Autumn, Cora and Victoria had the supper started, chili, the chili her father taught her and Ronnie to make. She packed some for Noah and Logan and took it over to them. She stopped at the jailhouse first. Noah was locking up a man for being drunk.

"Is he all right?"

"He just had too much to drink. He'll sleep it off. So what is it that brings you here and do I smell chili?"

"You do, with cornbread. I thought you might be hungry. I'm taking some to Logan too, I think he said he's working late tonight, paper work I believe."

"Yep, he's been so busy seeing patients he hasn't had time for the paperwork. So he picks one night to get caught up. I'm sure he'll appreciate the supper. I know I do, thanks."

Autumn left to take some to Logan, when she went inside his office he was working so hard he didn't even realize she was there. She cleared her throat then he looked up and saw her with a tray.

"Well hey, let me help you with that."

"It's fine I have it, I thought you might be hungry. I know you're busy so I won't stay but please enjoy the food. Don't work too late."

Then she left to go back to the saloon, when she was crossing the street she saw a man in the alley with a woman who looked scared and wanted out of there. She ran to get Noah for help.

"Noah come quickly, there is a man in the alley and the woman looks scared. I don't think she wants to be with him."

"I'll take care of it, you go back to the saloon."

Autumn did as she was told hoping Noah would get there before that man could hurt that woman. She went to get ready before Austin came to pick her up, she was excited about the horse for Ronnie and couldn't wait for him to see him.

Noah went to the alley and found the man ready to attack the woman, he pulled his gun from his holster.

"Hold it right there, put your hands up high, now."

He mentioned for the woman to run, she ran as fast as she could and went back home.

"Move it now. I'm taking you in so don't make any moves."

This man was a hard nosed dog. He was not well liked in town, always making advances towards the ladies.

"Reid don't you ever get tired of being told to leave these ladies alone?"

"What are ladies for if not to have a little fun with?"

"They aren't play things, their human beings. Let's go, I'm taking you in, move."

Reid turned as if to shoot Noah but Noah shot first. When he saw Reid had no gun he went over to him to see how bad he was. Noah got him in the heart.

"Why Reid, why did you did you pretend you were going to shoot me?"

Reid could barely breath, he was doing what he could to talk.

"Your brother...diagnosed me with yellow fever. I can't take the pain any more. I knew you wouldn't kill me on purpose, so it had to be this way."

Noah looked down at Reid, he couldn't think of a thing to say.

"Don't feel guilty...it's best this way."

Reid took his last breath, then he was gone. Noah picked him up and carried him to Logan's office. He told him what happened. Logan saw his brother's face.

> "He's right about one thing, don't feel guilty. This was how he was destined. Reid was suffering, you did do him a favor whether you did this intentionally or not. There was nothing that could be done. He told me he wanted to die, I didn't think he would go to such lengths to get there."

> "So he would have done anything to get himself killed?"

> "Yes he would, and did."

Noah didn't realize the pain he was in, but it didn't condone how he went about it, and it didn't make him feel any better. Noah walked to the door, opened it then stopped.

> "I'm going to dig a grave for him."

Logan stopped what he was doing and went with Noah. It was clear Noah would have a tough time of this, Logan wanted to be there for him.

> "Noah, you know this isn't your fault? He set you up. I know the pain he was in, unbearable. To be honest, I'm not surprised he did this."

> "That doesn't make it right."

> "No it doesn't, it just makes it what it is and you can't blame yourself."

Maybe now he could, but he knew it would wear off somewhere soon. Maybe in some strange way Noah could understand why he did what he did. He and Logan buried Reid, Noah made a cross for the head of the grave and carved Reid's name into it then carved the dates. Logan said a few words then he and Noah went to the jailhouse and had a shot of whiskey.

Autumn was just about ready knowing Austin would be coming soon. They seemed to enjoy each others company. She started down the stairs as beautiful as ever when Austin walked in and stood staring at her.

> "Nothing could possibly be more beautiful than you are right now."

> "Thank you, you look very handsome also."

> "The horse is hooked up to the buggy, we can take him to the ranch first."

"Oh yes, I can't wait to see him."

They went outside and there he was. He couldn't be more perfect, and black as night.

"Are you sure he was only one hundred dollars?"

"That's all."

"Ronnie will love this horse. Let's take him out, he'll be so surprised."

Austin helped her in the buggy, then he stepped up and they rode out to the ranch.

"Thank you for thinking about Ronnie, you didn't have to you know."

"I know, but to get right down to it I didn't, you did." "What? What do you mean?"

"Well you bought him for your brother, I didn't. I just told you about him."

He looked at her then chuckled, she started laughing with him. They enjoyed spending time together and getting to know each other. The ride to the ranch was peaceful and relaxing. Before long they were at the ranch, Autumn opened the barn and Austin took the horse inside and fed him before they left. Austin has strong feelings for Autumn whether she realized that or not, but maybe deep inside she didn't realize the feelings she has for him.

"That horse is beautiful, so black and shiny even. Ronnie will love him for sure."

Autumn was so taken by the horse, Austin believed she was in love with the horse herself.

"So I'm guessing you love horses too?"

"I always have, I use to have my own horse a long time ago, but it broke loose and never did come back home. I was heartbroken."

"Well maybe you can get one of your own and Ronnie could keep it here for you."

Autumn thought he was joking, then she saw his face.
"I don't think so, I have enough in my life right now. We'd better get going."

They rode back into town and had supper at the hotel, Austin ordered a bottle of wine for them to share.

> "Wine? Are we celebrating something?"

> "You might say that. A toast to us, and may our relationship continue to grow."

Autumn wasn't sure what he meant by that, but she was hoping things would grow between them. They did enjoy spending time together and he seemed to be a very nice man. He loved children and would do anything to help anyone. She just wasn't sure she was ready yet. He planned everything with impressions that he is getting serious.

> "Do you like the wine?"

> "Yes, it's delicious, candle light and atmosphere. Everything is wonderful."

They enjoyed their supper and the wine, each others company, everything was perfect. Maybe too perfect. After supper they went for a ride to the lake. Strolling along then they found a tree to sit under and just talk.

> "Autumn, if you hadn't noticed I am very taken by you. You're really a wonderful woman and I enjoy being with you."

At first she didn't know what to say.

> "I enjoy being with you, but Austin...I have some things I need to work out. I hope you can understand that."

He wasn't sure what she was trying to tell him.

> "So do you want me to stop seeing you? I'm not clear as to what you want."

> "No, I'm just asking if we could slow down some. You're a wonderful man and I want to be ready really I do, but I need to work somethings out first."

Austin seemed a little disappointed.

> "It's okay, I do understand. I don't want to rush you. Take all the the time you need, I can wait."

Chapter 6

Ronnie reached West Yellowstone, no matter where he was there were posters everywhere about the rodeo. He took one down and kept it in his pocket, someone approached him.

"You're new in town, haven't seen you here before?" Ronnie turned to see who was talking to him.

"That's right."

"Why did ya take that poster down? You aiming to enter that rodeo?"

"I am."

"Welcome to West Yellowstone boy, I'm Reid. If you're aiming to sign up for that there rodeo just head on over to the sheriff's office. Over yonder. Always looking for new blood in the rodeo. Makes it more of a challenge."

Ronnie looked in the man's eyes, it were as if he were the one challenging him. "Mighty grateful to ya, Reid. I'm Ronnie from Anaconda."

"Anaconda, you ain't that far, glad to meet ya."

They shook hands and Ronnie walked over to the sheriff's office. He walked in the door and shut it then stood there waiting for him, the sheriff came out from the back room.

"Something I can do for you stranger?"

"Ronnie, that's my name. I was told I can sign up for the rodeo here, is that right?"

The sheriff looked Ronnie over as he sat in his chair.

"You aiming to win that rodeo do ya?"

"I'm aiming, you didn't answer my question."

"Yep, this is where you sign."

He pulled the papers out of his drawer and set them in front of Ronnie with a pen.

"Here you go son."

"Sheriff I don't want to get off to a bad start here but I'm not your son. I'm just here for the rodeo."

"Now don't get huffy boy...Ronnie. Just aiming to be friendly."

Ronnie looked at him then sat down to fill out the papers.

"So where you from...Ronnie?"

"Does that matter for the rodeo?"

"Look, just trying to be friendly, seems you have a chip on your shoulder. That won't hold around here."

"Sorry, seems like people here are suspicious of out of towners."

They stared at each other before the sheriff spoke again.

"I get that and I am sorry about that. Last month we had a couple men in town not so friendly. They shot my brother, no reason."

Ronnie hung his head feeling ill.

"You all right?"

"About a month ago two men brutally murdered my parents. My sister and I moved to Anaconda to be with our cousins, why they killed them, we don't know. I can understand now why people are suspicious. I can tell you I ain't that kind. Just here for the rodeo."

The sheriff saw something in his face and he knew Ronnie was telling the truth.

"I'm sorry to hear that. Where bouts are you from originally?"

"Cheyenne Wyoming."

"Well now you may not believe this but we got word of that here. Really am sorry to hear that. Do you know who they were?"

"No, I wish I did, I'd hunt them down and shoot them like the dogs they are."

The sheriff knew how he felt, he couldn't help but wonder if those two men were the same two who killed his brother.

"I'm sheriff Clayton. Can't say I blame you but being sheriff..."

"Yeah I know. Don't worry, like I said I'm just here for the rodeo. Much obliged to ya."

Ronnie got up to leave when Clayton spoke to him.

"Ronnie, the hotel across the street is a good place to stay while you're here. Tell Maggie at the desk I sent ya, she'll make a good deal. If you need anything, just let me know."

"Well thank you. I'll do that."

Ronnie went across the road to get a room, the rodeo was the next day, he was anxious to win that two thousand dollar prize.

"I'm here for a room please, Sheriff Clayton sent me."

"You're not from around here how do you know the sheriff?"

"I just came from his office, I'm in town for the rodeo. Is there a problem?"

Maggie looked up and saw Clayton in the door way.

"No problem, just being careful is all. Sign here, your room is upstairs first door on the right. Welcome."

Ronnie picked up the key nodded to her then went on upstairs. Maggie just looked at the sheriff.

"So what's the story sheriff?"

"Maggie, remember hearing about the couple in Cheyenne that was murdered?"

"Yep."

"That couple was his parents. Two men, can't help but wonder if they're the Bart brother's. Didn't tell him that, he's still hurting. Sure wouldn't be surprised if they were. Go easy easy on him Maggie, he's a good man."

Maggie looked up the stairs and then hung her head.

"Why do you think it was the brothers?"

"We talked, just from what he told me." Maggie agreed to go easy on him.

"Shame sheriff, will it ever end? Those brothers need to be stopped."

"Some day soon, I hope."

The sheriff leaves and goes back to the jailhouse. Ronnie is in his room settling in, he takes out a picture of his parents and sets in on the bed side table then sits and talks to them.

"I'm gonna win that prize tomorrow and I'll have a fine ranch. You'll see. Autumn and I will be fine, I'll see to that."

He laid back on the bed for a spell after his trip into town. He fell asleep for a while with the rodeo on his mind. His father once entered a rodeo and won. He only went once when Ronnie was a small boy, it was how he got his ranch started. It was a memory Ronnie won't soon forget, then he was waken by a shot. He jumped off he bed and looked out the window. Someone just shot a snake. There was a knock on his door.

"Who is it?"

"It's Maggie, I thought you might be hungry, brought you something to eat."

He opened the door and there she stood with a tray.

"Thank you but I didn't order any food.."

"Well you gotta eat, you've been here most of the day and haven't been down so I brought you something. Enjoy."

"That's kind of you, thank you."

Ronnie took the tray and sat on the bed eating what she brought him. Maybe the people here are friendly, just had a bad time, no one understood that like Ronnie. His father taught him how to ride in a rodeo like he did. If he won this rodeo it would be for him. Suddenly Ronnie heard Maggie scream, he ran downstairs and found a man grabbing a her. He pulled out his gun.

"Leave her go."

The man looked up a him.

"Mind your business boy." Ronnie shot him in his arm.

"I said back off."

Sheriff Clayton heard the shot and came running in to see what happened.

"What's going on here?"

Maggie was just about in tears.

"He came in and grabbed me, if it weren't for Ronnie there's no telling what he would have done to me."

"Okay let's go, I'm putting you in jail."

"He shot me! What about my arm?"

"Don't worry the doc will tend to you, you need to learn some manners in this town."

He looked at Ronnie and tipped his hat. Maggie was so glad Ronnie was there.

"How can I thank you?"

"No need, just making sure you're safe. You okay Maggie?"

"I am now, thank you a heap, I'm grateful."

Ronnie went back to his room cleaned up and brought the tray back downstairs.

"Can you spare about half an hour?"

Maggie looked at him wondering what was on his mind.

"I suppose I can, why?"

"Thought I'd buy you a drink, relax a bit at the saloon. Calm your nerves some. Just being friendly, no one should go through what you just did. That's no way to treat a lady. No intentions, just thought you could use a drink."

Maggie smiled, no one ever asked her for a drink before. "Why that's mighty kind of you, I'd like that."

She set out her sign and walked over to the saloon with Ronnie.

"So have you lived in this town long?"

Maggie was flattered, no one has ever taken an interest in her before.

"All my life. My parents own a ranch not far from here. They're good folk, we're close. I just always had my mind set on my own business."

"My sister has her own business, she bought the saloon in Anaconda. Me, I wanted my own ranch. Just bought one, needs repairs but not too bad. I have two horses and a rooster. Darn thing wakes me at the crack of dawn."

They shared a laugh together as they walked in the saloon. They sat at a table and Ronnie went to the bar and paid for their drinks, then brought them back and sat down so they could talk.

"You know it's not that I mind getting up at the crack of dawn but there are days when sleeping in a while would be great. No matter that's what ranch life is about."

"No one has ever been this kind to me before. Thank you."

Ronnie looked at her, she was a beautiful young woman and he couldn't imagine anyone not showing her an interest.

"If you don't mind me saying I can't believe no one would take a shine to you. As pretty as you are?"

"Yeah well, thank you anyway."

"Tell you what, how about after the rodeo I buy you some supper. I sure wouldn't mind the company."

Maggie felt a blush but agreed, she never gets out with male company and Ronnie seemed so kind.

"You're very kind thank you. I accept your generous invitation."
"Then we're set. Would you like another drink?"

"Thank you but I really should be getting back to the hotel. I am feeling so much better now."

Ronnie was glad to hear that and he walked her back to the hotel.

> "Thank you for the drink, you really should be getting some rest for the rodeo tomorrow, you want to be alert and ready."

> "You're right, but if you need anything, help or such, come and get me I'm not far."

Maggie thanked him and assured him she should be fine. He went up to his room and turned in early for the night. He lay in bed for a while thinking about Autumn, Logan and Noah. He thought about his ranch and how if he won that money he could make it as he had always dreamed he would. The room was getting hot so he cracked open the window for some fresh air, soon after he was asleep.

Maggie did peek in on him to make sure he had everything he needed but found him sleeping.

> "Good night dear one, thank you so much for everything. You are a true gentleman."

She blew him a kiss then closed his door so he could sleep. Maggie went back downstairs to lock up for the night then turned in herself. For sure she would attend the rodeo if only to wish Ronnie well, he deserved at least that much. If he wins that would be the best, Maggie really had no way to pay him back so winning this event would be wonderful for him.

The next morning Maggie was up very early, she fixed breakfast for Ronnie. Ham eggs and pancakes, he would need his strength to win. She carried the tray up to his room and knocked on his door.

> "Who's there?"

> "It's Maggie, I wanted to wish you luck in the rodeo. I'm sure you'll do fine. Be careful."

With that she kissed him on his cheek then ran off back downstairs, she had guests to tend to, people cam to town if only for the rodeo. Ronnie came downstairs, checked on Maggie and she wished him well. Then he went to the stable for his horse and was on his way. Maggie found someone to fill in for her, she wanted to go and watch Ronnie in the rodeo. Maggie went to the stable and got into her buggy and on she went.

When she arrived the place was filled, not an empty seat anywhere. After walking around a man offered her his seat, she thanked him then sat down waiting to see Ronnie. They started off with barrel racing, both men and women racing around the barrels in a cloverleaf fashion each one trying to be the fastest racer. There were a couple of close numbers but the winner was a woman, Annie Gains. She was a champion barrel racer.

Bareback riding was next, Ronnie was first to come out riding. Maggie was very impressed, she's never seen anyone ride like he did. There were three other men who entered the bareback riding and only one came close to Ronnie, but Ronnie did win. The roping event was next, again Ronnie and three others tried their best. Ronnie was last this time, Maggie was sitting there hoping he would make it again. She knows how much his ranch means to him. Ronnie slipped when he dismounted his horse but still managed to rope the calf. Because of that slip he tied with another contestant.

Before the last event of the rodeo a clown entered the ring, walking around with a cigar in his mouth, the announcer saw him.

> "What's that clown doing in the ring get him out of there, he could get hurt."

The clown stood there and looked at him.

> "I could get hurt, you're putting everyone to sleep. What do you know about rodeos?"

The announcer looked at him and stood up.

> "I'll have you know I use to ride in rodeos. I'm a genuine cowboy."

> "Oh you use to be a cowboy, wouldn't that make you deranged?"

The announcer turned red in anger.

> "Ladies and gentlemen, this person who calls himself an announcer is an ex-cowboy. I call him a dinosaur at the rodeo, you know, a bronco-saurus."

The crowed was laughing, all having a good time. The announcer once again cries out to get him out of there, but the clown continues.

> "Hey folks, what do you call a rodeo bull with a sense of humor? Laughing stock."

This clown wasn't stopping for anything. Once again the announcer called out to him.

"Hey you bag of fruit, you better get out of the ring they are releasing
a bull now."

The clown turned and saw they opened the chute. He began running in the ring while the bull went after him. There was a barrel where the clown jumped into.

"Hey you dumb bag of bones, why don't you go see a butcher?"

The bull charged towards him, the clown got down in the barrel and the bull hit bucked the barrel around the ring, the crowed was on the edge of their seats wondering what was going to happen. After a few bucks the announcer came into the ring to distract the bull while the clown got out of the barrel and out of the ring. The announcer then followed. The crowed stood and cheered clapping their hands. The announcer went back to the stand and announced the final event.

"Thank you ladies and gentlemen and now for the final event of the
rodeo. The winner of this event will take home two thousand dollars
for wrestling a steer to the ground. This can be a dangerous one if they
aren't careful, but all the contestants are very skilled and know what
they are doling. So before we start let's give them a round of applause."

The crowed again stood up and applauded and cheered. The final round, steer wrestling. The first contestant fell, the clown came out right away to distract the steer while two other men came out to carry the injured man out of the ring.

"Ladies and gentlemen lucky for this man he is not seriously hurt, he
will be fine. We hate to see anyone get hurt but it can happen."

Ronnie was last, two out of the other three men tied, now it was up to Ronnie. They released the steer and opened the gate for Ronnie. The crowed watched as Ronnie chased the steer jumped from his horse grabbed the horns of the steer and wrestled him to the ground. Time was called and the crowed waited for the results. Ronnie won, ten point seven seconds. He came out on the field and the crowed cheered, when he turned to his right to leave the grounds he saw Maggie standing and clapping with a huge smile on her face. He waved to her and smiled back, what a surprise it was to see her there.

After it was over he went to her and offered to take her home. "Thank
you, I'd like that."

"You never told me you were coming, I would have brought you."

"I wanted it to be a surprise." Ronnie smiled.

"It sure was, thank you for coming."

"I knew you would win."

"Oh you did?"

"Yes, I saw the determination in your eyes, anyone with that much determination is bound to win."

Ronnie nodded his head, they had a peaceful ride home. They talked and became acquainted and just enjoyed what was left of the day and each others company. When they arrived back in town Ronnie rode the buggy to the stable as well as his horse and he and Maggie walked back to the hotel, they said good night then went to their rooms and to bed. He couldn't believe he won the money, he had hoped to but didn't really count on winning. For a short while Ronnie gazed out the window up at the sky packed full of stars.

"Mom, dad, I know you can see me and I can't believe I actually won. I'll have my ranch and it will be what I want it to be. Thanks for all you taught me, it was a heap of helping and I heard all you tried to tell me, I love you."

After that he went to bed, he was exhausted and a little sore. He couldn't wait for Autumn and Logan and Noah to hear about this. In the morning he would be leaving after he bought something for his sister and cousins, maybe a little something for Maggie. Right now all he wanted was a good nights sleep.

Maggie was in bed thinking about the day she had and how wonderful it was. It was a day she won't forget, there was one thing she wanted to do before she went sleep. She had to take care of it tonight, it couldn't wait, then she would be able to sleep.

When dawn broke the light shone through the window waking Ronnie. How nice it was to wake up by light and not by rooster, but he would have to get use to that having his own ranch. Maybe Maggie would join him for breakfast, he cleaned up and was dressed in no time and looking forward to seeing her. He rushed down to her room and knocked, but there was no answer. Looking around he could tell she hasn't been out of her room yet, certain things were done when she was up, but there was no sign of her being up and around. Once again he knocks on the door, this time he opened the door calling her name. She never answered, he went in to see her still in bed. Ronnie walked over to her and tried to wake her, but there was no response of any kind.

Maggie felt cold, he checked for a pulse, there was none. Quickly he opened her window and saw the sheriff. He called out for him for help.

"Sheriff Clayton, get over here now with a doctor, fast."

The sheriff ran to the doctors office and they ran over to the hotel where Ronnie met them. He told them what he found as they went into Maggie's room. The doctor went over and checked on her, he pronounced her dead. Ronnie didn't understand what happened.

"There has to be a reason, a person just doesn't go to bed and not wake up, what happened?"

The sheriff and the doctor just looked at each other, that confirmed they knew what happened.

"Dang it tell me."

Ronnie was angry and wanted answers now. The doctor saw Ronnie's face and he knew right then he cared for Maggie.

"Mr. Snyder, I'm Doctor Porter. Maggie was one of my patients. Several months back she came to me, not feeling well at all. I had diagnosed her with tuberculosis, she knew she would die but didn't want anyone to know. She wanted to live her life without anyone treating her differently because of this."

Ronnie was stunned, he sat down staring in disbelief. The sheriff happened to notice a letter with his name on it, he picked it up.

"I think she left this for you."

He opened the letter and began to read. The letter read:

Dearest Ronnie, I hope you can forgive me for not telling you about my illness, we were having such a good time I didn't want to spoil that. I appreciate you helping me and coming to my defense when I was in trouble, and I thank you for a lovely time. You were the best one in the rodeo, I just knew you would win. I hope now that your ranch will be what you want it to be, you're a wonderful man and deserve the best life has to offer you. Don't be afraid to grab it whatever it may be. Take care of yourself, I couldn't be more happy to have met you. You showed me great joy before I left this world and I will always be grateful to you for that. Enjoy your life while you can. Affectionally, Maggie.

As Ronnie read the letter tears rolled down his face. He couldn't speak, he just stood up and left with the letter she left for him. The sheriff and the doctor knew this wasn't good. Sheriff Clayton left following Ronnie to keep an eye on him, he was in a fragile state right now. He followed Ronnie to his room and saw him pull out a bottle of whiskey.

"Do you think that will help?"

Ronnie turned to find him standing in his doorway.
"Not entirely, but it can take the pain away for a while."

He poured a glass and with one gulp had it down quickly, he laid the letter on the dresser.

"I saw the two of you together, she really cared about you. I'm sure you cared about her too just by your actions."

Still Ronnie didn't talk just poured another glass of whiskey. "Does she have any family?"

"She never did say, I can't be sure."

He was angry right now and the sheriff understood that. Sheriff Clayton walked out the door telling Ronnie he would be back later to check on him. Again he read the letter once more, then laid down on the bed. It wasn't right, not having someone in their life just wasn't right. The doctors voice was coming from downstairs, Ronnie could hear him. He went downstairs to talk to him about the arrangements.

"She will be taken care of tomorrow."

He wanted to be a part of it, help in any way he could. The next day at the burial Ronnie was there, he couldn't believe she was gone. Maggie is someone he will not soon forget. On her grave he laid a bouquet of roses, she deserved them. The sheriff came up behind Ronnie.

"I know you'll be leaving very soon. I found this in her personal things and thought you might like to have this. I'm sure she would want you to have this."

Ronnie took what the sheriff offered to him, a picture of Maggie. He took the picture and put it in his wallet, thanked the sheriff then left for home. West Yellowstone would be nothing but a bittersweet memory for him, a start and a finish in one visit.

Autumn was at his ranch taking care of the horse she bought for her brother and taking care of things around the ranch. Austin had stopped by to help anyway he could, she couldn't wait for Ronnie to see the horse.

"Thank you Austin for your help I do appreciate everything you've done."

"It's not much really. The orphanage is coming along, they will probably have it done much sooner than they planned."

"I've seen it, the progress is incredible. Things seem to be going very well. The orphanage and Ronnie's ranch. I can't wait to see his face when he see's this horse."

Later that afternoon Ronnie came riding into town, Sally was the first to see him and came running out to meet him.

"Mr. Ronnie, you're back. We missed you."

Ronnie jumped down from his horse and picked up Sally hugging her tight.

"I missed all of you too Sally. Have you been a good girl while I was away?"

"Yes sir, I was. Ask Miss Autumn." Autumn came rushing out to see her brother.

"It's good to have you back home. You must be hungry."

"No I'm good. I just wanted to see everyone before I go home."

She knew something was bothering him.

"Well would you mind if I went to the ranch with you?"

"Don't you have a saloon to run?"

"Just for a short spell. I need to show you some things."

Ronnie wasn't much in the mood but he knew she would be insistent.

Autumn sent Sally to the jail house while she kept Ronnie busy, Sally knew to make Logan and Noah aware that Ronnie was back and to go out to the ranch to welcome Ronnie home. While she handled that Autumn walked Ronnie over to the orphanage so he could see the progress they were making. Arjun turned and saw his friend, he saw in his face something was wrong. He and Ronnie walked off to the side so Ronnie could explain to him what happened while he was away.

"My friend, I understand your pain. Your sister has a surprise in store for you, that is why I am keeping you here. Later this evening I will come to your ranch and I will help you through this. My promise to you."

"Thank you my friend, you will be most welcomed."

Ronnie held his head down and Arjun saw Autumn and others in a wagon going to the ranch.

> "Shortly I am to take you to your ranch. I promise you I will help
> you through this. For now, your sister awaits a surprise. We should
> go now."

Ronnie couldn't imagine what Autumn had in store for him but he did as Arjun had asked, he didn't want to disappoint his sister. They rode slowly out to the ranch while Ronnie told Arjun about his trip and how it ended. Arjun had hoped that his sisters plan would lift his spirits even a little. They were approaching the ranch but Ronnie saw no one in site.

> "Where is she?"

> "I am to take you inside the barn. You will see."

When they dismounted their horses they walked into the barn so Ronnie could take his horse inside, when he opened the barn doors there he found his sister, Austin, Tim and Victoria, Logan and Nosh, Marsha and Cora.

> "What is going on and where did that horse come from?"

Autumn walked over to him and hugged him.

> "I bought him for you, isn't he a beaut? I couldn't pass him by he is
> such a beautiful horse."

Ronnie looked the horse over, not a thing wrong with him. He couldn't have picked a better one if he tried.

> "He looks like he cost a fortune."

> "Not really, Austin found the horse I just bought him."

Austin stepped into the conversation.

> "The man she bought him from couldn't afford to keep him, but he
> wanted to sell the horse to someone who would take good care of him.
> I knew you would so he gave Autumn a great price."

Ronnie couldn't speak, between the horse and everything he's been through, only Arjun knew what a comfort it was to have everyone there right now. Marsha went over to Ronnie and welcomed him home with a hug.

"Well for this occasion I baked a cake, what if we all go inside and cut it, there's fresh coffee on the stove."

They all went inside, except Ronnie. He couldn't tear himself away from the horse. Arjun walked over and put his hand on his shoulder.

"We should go inside, they will start to wonder."

He was right, Ronnie wasn't ready just yet to explain things. They went inside and Marsha cut the cake while Autumn served the coffee. Noah was curious about Ronnie's trip.

"So how did things go in West Yellowstone?"

"Well I won the money in the rodeo so I can move on with making this ranch the way I hoped it would be."

Autumn was happy.

"You won! How wonderful, mom and dad would be so proud. We are too, I knew you could win."

Ronnie changed the subject of conversation, he didn't want to talk too much about his trip.

"So how soon do you think the orphanage will be completed?"

Logan thought a moment.

"Well by the end of this week, wouldn't you say Noah?"

Noah agreed, everyone was in good moods and things were all coming together. Austin pulled out his harmonica and everyone enjoyed themselves, most everyone. Ronnie poured another cup of coffee and went out on the porch, Arjun followed.

"You know my friend, your cousin is going through his own struggle. Maybe it would help you to help him if you can."

"If I can? I would do anything to help him, what's wrong?"

"His situation is similar to yours. A man named Reid had a fatal disease, he was going to die and he knew it. This Reid was suffering

155

very bad pain and couldn't take it anymore. He tricked Noah into shooting him so he wouldn't have to deal with his illness."

"How did he trick Noah into shooting him?"

"He pretended he had a gun and he was going to shoot him. Noah didn't know what happened until after he thought he was defending himself. He's been miserable since then. The doctor told him why he did what he did..."

"I know, it didn't make it any easier. Thank you for telling me."

Noah walked out on the porch.

"Hey what's going on, this party is for you?"

"You're right, let's get back in there, we can't let them have all the fun."

Arjun nodded and smiled at Ronnie, they all went back in to celebrate. They were singing and dancing, it was good to be around such joy. Time was going by so quick, Marsha stood up to say something.

"Well this has been a delightful trip, Autumn with the saloon and Ronnie with his ranch. I miss all of you but it's good to see your dreams come true. However I do have to get back home. Things won't take care of themselves. I can promise you I will be back again. I love you all and even though I'm miles away you're all still my family here. Tomorrow is my last day here, I'll be leaving on the evening train."

Everyone was sorry to see her go, it was great to see her again. Autumn, Austin and everyone began to leave. The night was getting late and tomorrow things were back to normal. Arjun hung back until everyone was gone. Then he and Ronnie went outside.

"Do you have a personal item of Maggie's?"

"Yes, she left me two of her pictures. Here is one."

Arjun took the picture and pulled a small handful of sweet grass from his pocket kept in a buckskin pouch. He lit the grass with fire to burn it and held the picture over it to purify. Then he wrapped in the buckskin pouch. Arjun and Ronnie sat and smoked a sacred pipe.

"Now we smoke this pipe for Maggie. She did not die but is walking on to continue her journey. Free from pain and suffering."

They passed the pipe to each other to signify her journey.

> "Now you are to keep this bundle in a special place, and vow to live a harmonious life till the soul is released. This will be a year after which you will carry the bundle outside and as soon as it reaches the air, her soul will be released."

Ronnie looked into the sky grateful to have known her.

> "Thank you my friend. I'm happy to be able to call you my friend, and proud."

> "I feel the same. I came here for a purpose, seems like I was more useful than I had expected to be. You know where you can find me if ever you need me. I'm never far away. I've been gone a long time now, my friends and I need to return to our tribe."

> "Thank you, I hope we meet again."

> "We will. Take care."

With that Arjun jumped on his horse and left to get his friends and go back home.

Chapter 7

The next day all was well and back to normal. The building was close to complete, Ronnie won the rodeo prize money to get his ranch going, Autumn was doing very well with the saloon. Ronnie walked in the saloon with Logan, Noah, Sally and Austin. Cora saw them walk in, she just wasn't sure if it would be good or bad.

> "Autumn, I think you need to get out there. All your family and even Austin and Sally are here. Victoria and Tim are with them."

She wasn't sure herself what to expect, she left the kitchen to find out if something was wrong.

> "What happened? What's wrong?"

> "Relax nothing is wrong. I had everyone meet me here for a reason. Get Cora out here."

Cora heard and came right out.

"Now that everyone is here I want to say thank you for being here and to tell everyone of you, that I do love all of you. Each of you are special to me in your own ways and I'm very lucky to have all of you in my life. Now that the big stuff is out of the way, Sally would you please help me?"

"Sure, what should I do?"

"You see this bag? I'm going to hand you things from it and tell you who to give it too. Can you do that for me?"

"I sure can."

He would take out a package from the bag hand it to Sally and she would give it to whoever he told her to, she felt very important. Once every package was given Ronnie told them to open them.

"Wait a minute, here is one I forgot to out in the bag. Sally, this is for you."

"Oh boy, thank you."

Ronnie explained after the rodeo he went shopping for everyone, it was his way of celebrating. They were all very pleased with what Ronnie gave them, but they all explained it wasn't necessary.

"It is necessary, to me. I care about every one of you."

With that being said he turned and left to go back to his ranch. Autumn was curious, he was strange somehow.

"Noah, what's going on I've never seen him this way?"

"I really don't know, I'm sure when he's ready he will tell us, if there is anything going on."

"Noah is right, if something is wrong he will tell us on his own, but what is wrong with his buying gifts?"

"It's not that Logan, it's something about his attitude. I can't explain it but it's a feeling."

Maybe Logan was right, maybe nothing is wrong. Tim knocked on the table for everyone's attention.

"Excuse me, I don't mean to cut in but Victoria and I have something we'd like to share with you. Go ahead dear."

"Well like Tim said we have some news. Tim and I found out we're going to have a baby."

Everyone was excited for them, what wonderful news. Autumn hugged them both.

"Drinks for everyone, and a sarsaparilla for the mother to be, and Sally."

Autumn seemed a little detached, she went back to the kitchen for a moment. Austin was right behind her, he was concerned.

"Autumn, are you all right?"

"Yes I'm fine, thank you."

"You're not, I can tell."

He knew her as if he knew her all his life.

"Honestly I'm just a bit preoccupied is all. Really."

"All right I'll accept that for now, but later we need to talk."

What was she going to tell him, whatever she would tell him he would understand, he always has. So much has happened the past few months and it all has her thinking. Maybe she wanted a little more from life, what was going to make her truly happy? She's been keeping so busy she wasn't sure herself anymore. Maybe she should talk things over with Austin, maybe he could help her sort things out. Why should she be dependent on him, how would that be fair to him? Victoria went into the kitchen looking for Autumn.

"Austin we can talk...Victoria! I'm sorry I thought you were Austin."
"Forget it, I came to see if you need any help."

Victoria took one look at her and she knew she needed help of a different kind. "Would you like to talk?"

159

"I don't know what's wrong with me, Austin is a wonderful man. I can't remember anything about my parents murders, it feels like I lost a piece of my life. I'm so confused."

"Confused? Look at the work you've done for the orphans. A confused person couldn't have done that. What about the help you gave to people in this town, you're running this saloon and still find time for others. I don't think you're confused, scared maybe."

Autumn looked at her as if she didn't understand anything she said.

"Scared? What have I got to be scared about?"

"Commitment with Austin. It seems to me that you lost important things in your life. Your parents, home, and I'm sure your friends in Cheyenne. I think you're afraid of losing Austin or maybe being hurt if you do. Tim and I both see how he feels about you, I really don't believe he would hurt you. Not intentionally. He cares for you more than anything."

Everything she said, could it really be that way? "Maybe, I'm not sure."

"Let go and let him in, you'll see for yourself the happiness I know he wants to give you. Don't let it slip away, take a chance. You won't be sorry and if you don't, you'll always wonder what could have been."

Victoria left her with those thoughts. It was a lot to think about, but Autumn knew she was right. She wasn't really moving on with her life, just everyone else's. No one but she could make that change. Autumn left a note in the kitchen, she needed some time to think about things and not to worry, she would be fine and be back soon. Cora went in the kitchen and found the note after she heard the back door shut. She rushed out of the kitchen to the others.

"Autumn is gone. She left this note, it says please do not worry she'll be fine and will be back soon. She needed some time to herself. What should we do?"

Austin was worried.

"I'm going to look for her now." Victoria knew she would be fine.

160

"Wait Austin, she will be fine. Please, let her have the time she asks for. All she wants is some time to sort through some thoughts. Autumn will be back and she will be fine."

"How can you be sure?"

"I can't explain how but I can promise you, she will."

Autumn went to the stable to get a buggy and take a ride to the lake. It was peaceful there, quiet and she could relax and sort through things. She went for a stroll by the lake, the sunlight reflecting on the water. The trees blowing in the gentle breeze. As she was walking along the edge she was feeling free and happy when she stepped on something and lost her balance. Autumn fell into the lake, she was panicked and felt as though she were drowning. A hand reached into the water and pulled her out. When she turned to thank the person she froze.

The person who pulled her out was her mother! How, how could that be.

"Don't be frightened, it is me but only you can see me. I've been with you all the time, I never left you. I know you're struggling about Austin."

"Mom, I can't believe you're here."

"I don't have much time so please listen. He is a good man and he can make you happy. Don't be afraid, if you give into your fear you will miss out on happiness. I will always be with you and Ronnie."

"Wait, please don't go!"

"I have to, I can't stay. I love you both."

She blew a kiss to Autumn and vanished. She sat down and cried seeing her mother then losing her again. Only not really, she did say she is always with them. That is when things became clear to her, she now understands things much better. Autumn ran back to the buggy and went as fast as she could to get back to the saloon. It was true, everything Victoria and her mother told her, everything.

Autumn jumped down from the buggy and rushed inside. Cora was cleaning the bar.

"Where is Austin?" "Here I am."

He came out of the kitchen, he was fixing the table leg.

"What happened to you? Where were you."

"I was at the lake, I slipped and fell in but forget that. Would you like to go for a buggy ride? I need to change of course but...would you?"

He couldn't help but laugh, she looked touching.

"I would like that very much."

"I'll go change and be right down. Don't go away."

She certainly seemed enthusiastic about something, he couldn't wait to find out what. Austin finished what he needed to in the kitchen so he sat at a table with a beer while waiting for Autumn. It wasn't much longer she came downstairs as quickly as she could. When he saw her he couldn't take his eyes off of her.

"One more detail, I'll be back."

Autumn went into the kitchen to pack a picnic basket to take with them. There was food pretty much ready to pack, she even packed a bottle of wine.

"I'm ready now, I packed a basket to take along."

Austin was very curious right now.

"So what is going on?"

"No no, not just yet. Wait till we get to the lake."

They left together, he carried the basket then they got in the buggy and headed for the lake. Ronnie just happened to see them leaving smiling and so happy. This is good for her, for him it may take some time.

Austin drove the buggy then suddenly stopped.

"Is something wrong?"

"Not at all, I just thought maybe we could take Sally with us."

"If you don't mind, not this time. I really need to talk with you."

"This sounds important?"

"It is, could we please go now?"

Austin tugged at the reins and they were on their way to the lake. Ronnie went into the general store, he pulled out his keys and noticed the key chain. Billy came to mind, he made the chain for him. Ronnie promised to send him pictures of Anaconda. He also promised he would go back someday to visit him. Now maybe a good time for that.

As he walked through the general store looking around he found the picture post cards he promised to him. Ronnie picked out a few then continued to look around to see what he needed when he came across a toy horse, it looked just like the horse Autumn bought for him. That was it, the gift he would take to Billy. Tim Birescik walked in the store and saw Ronnie.

"Hey Ronnie, how is everything?" Ronnie looked up and saw Tim.

> "Hey Tim, things are good. I was just picking up some post cards and this toy horse. Looks just like my horse, the one Autumn bought."

> "Well look at that, you're right. Spitting image. So what the real one isn't enough for you?"

Tim was laughing joking with Ronnie.

> "It's not that, there's a little boy back in Cheyenne, his name is Billy I was kind of like a big brother to him. I promised him I would send him some picture post cards and bring him a gift when I go back to visit." Tim took one look at his face and he felt like Ronnie was a little home sick.

> "He lives with his father, he has no mother, they've had a hard life. I use to do whatever I could to help them. I took one look at these post cards and I started thinking about him."

> "So are you planning another trip?"

> "Not right now, maybe later. I'm going to box this up and send it to him. I think he would get a kick out of getting a package through the mail. I'll save the visit for another time."

Tim could see how important Billy is to him.

> "Well Billy is a lucky little boy to have a big brother like you. I know your not brothers by blood, but that doesn't mean much." "Hate to rush but I am in kind of a hurry. I'll see you around Tim."

Ronnie finished his business then left to wrap up the package and send it off to Billy. He could almost see how excited he would be when he gets the package.

At the lake Autumn and Austin were enjoying the picnic food she packed for them. She was in a very good mood.

"All right, I waited long enough. You look like you're ready to bust. What's going on?"

Autumn smiled so hard she thought she would bust.

"Remember our talk, about us? I said we should take things slow."

"Yes I do remember, I don't think I've been pressing you?"

"No you haven't, I've been doing a lot of thinking and I changed my mind. So many people losing their spouses, parents, family members of any kind. It's so sad."

"Yes it is, but what does that have to do with us?"

"I'm not saying it will but something could happen to either of us and then what? One of us could lose the other, we wouldn't have the pleasure of being together and knowing each other. It could all be over like that. Look at Etta's husband, neither of them knew when he went to work that day that he would never come home again."

Austin didn't know what to say, what happened to her? Maybe she hit her head? "Don't you think you're being a little gloomy?"

"No not at all. Think about it, what happened to her husband was an accident and could happen to anyone. I don't want anything like that happening to us. We should enjoy our time together, not waste a moment of happiness. Life is too short and you never know what could happen."

She leaned over and kissed him with passion, wanting him to know how she really feels now.

"I don't know what happened to you but I'm liking this. I'm really glad you changed your mind."

Austin hugged her so tight, he didn't want to let her go.

"I have something for you."

He reached in his pocket and pulled out a small box. Autumns face was glowing and her eyes filled with tears.

"Go on, open it."

When she opened the box she found a beautiful diamond ring.

"Oh Austin, I don't know what to say. It's the most beautiful ring I've ever seen, but how did you..."

"I didn't know anything. I've been carrying it around with me in case you would change your mind, and you did."

He took her hand and on one knee he looked into her eyes.

"My sweetest Autumn, love of my life. Will you do me the honor of becoming my wife?"

Tears began to pour down her face, she could barely breath right.

"I would be honored to become your wife, yes."

They both were so happy they couldn't let go of one another.

"I feel like the luckiest man alive."

They enjoyed what was left of the day, the sun was beginning to set. Begun to pack things up and Austin put the basket in the buggy and helped Autumn up, then he jumped up in and they started out for home. He drove slowly so they made it back a bit late. Austin walked Autumn to her door and they kissed goodnight.

Autumn couldn't believe she was engaged to be married, her ring was so beautiful. She had changed into her night clothes and opened her window just a bit. Then she hopped into bed, looked out the window and began to talk to her mother.

"Mom, you were right, you always were. I can't believe how happy I am. Thank you, I love you and dad too. Good night."

Autumn went to sleep still smiling and happy as she has been in what seemed like a very very long time.

At Ronnie's ranch he was in bed, thoughts racing through his mind. Some about Billy and some about Maggie. Billy and his father struggled through their lives together, their lives were hard yet they still seemed happy. Maggie was still a young woman who's time was cut short, it just didn't seem fair.

Soon Ronnie drifted off to sleep, troubled with his thoughts. The night seemed long and not so peaceful, tossing and turning. It was the middle of the night when a gust of wind blew through the window, Ronnie felt a heavy chill and pulled the blanket over him. Then he felt something he never expected, someone kissed him.

"What! Who's there?"

When he looked towards the window there stood Maggie. "Maggie... it can't be!"

"It is me Ronnie. I had to come and see you. You were always so nice to me I just had to come. You're friendship means so much to me, I wanted you to know that. I wish I could stay but I can't'

"Wait don't leave."

"You will always be in my heart. Take care Ronnie."

He sat up in bed breathing heavy and calling out to Maggie.

"It must have been a dream, it had to be."

He couldn't get back to sleep so he got out of bed and went to the living room.

"You are at peace now, just like Arjun said you would be."

Ronnie looked out the window into the sky, clear as any he saw a star shining extra bright and a a little bigger than the others.

"I know that one is you Maggie. Take care."

Ronnie went back to bed feeling a bit more at ease. Only this night was just beginning. There was a stranger lurking around the grounds quiet so he wouldn't wake Ronnie. It was at that moment Autumn was sleeping restlessly, she began tossing and turning.

"Autumn, wake up, please." "What? Who's there?"

When she sat up in bed she saw a woman standing at the foot of her bed, only it wasn't her mother.

"My name is Maggie, I know Ronnie. He is in trouble you need to go and get to his ranch immediately. Please before something terrible happens."

Autumn felt sick in her stomach, the woman who was there is now gone. She couldn't take any chances she had to get Noah. She got out of bed and put on her shawl then ran over to Noah's house. Pounding on the door and calling his name he answered the door and saw how frantic she was.

"I can't explain it but Ronnie is in trouble, please we need to go to his ranch quickly!"

"I'll get dressed, you go and get Logan."

Autumn did as Noah requested. Pounding on his door she told him the same thing.

"Slow down, how do you know he's in trouble?"

"I can't explain it but please hurry, Noah is on his way out there."

Logan got dressed and also headed out to Ronnie's ranch, he wasn't far behind Noah. When they arrived they saw a man entering his house. "Noah do you think that's Ronnie?"

"I can't tell from here, we better find out."

Slowly and quietly they approached his house when they heard a man's voice, but it wasn't Ronnie's.

"Well well, if it isn't Mr. tough guy coming to the rescue. You're not so tough now are you? What's the matter, your gun isn't handy? You should have minded your own business but you can't do that can you. From now on you won't have to concern yourself with being the tough guy."

"I remember you, you were the one who was attacking Maggie."

"What a shame, someone as smart as you going to waste. Well goodnight buddy boy."

There was a shot but not from Ronnie. The man fell to the floor bleeding from his back, when Ronnie looked up he saw Noah and Logan.

"How did you two know I needed help?"

Noah looked at Logan then at Ronnie.

> "I think a better question is how did Autumn know? She came to my place beating down the door."

Logan told him the same thing.

> "Noah sent her to my place so we could come out here, like he said beating down the door. She said she couldn't explain how she knew, she just did."

Noah nodded in agreement.

> "If you have anyone to thank it would be Autumn."

Ronnie helped them carry this man out to Logan's wagon, they took him to town and the next morning prepared a grave for him. Ronnie went to see Autumn, he wanted to know how she knew.

> "A woman named Maggie came to see me, she told me to get help an go to you. Who is Maggie?"

Ronnie felt a chill go down his spine. He and Autumn sat down while Ronnie explained everything to her, almost everything.

> "I'm so sorry Ronnie, I'm sure she cared a great deal for you. Why else would she be looking out for you."

> "Since we moved to Anaconda, I have heard about ghosts hanging around here. I have to say I never believed one of any of it, but after tonight I may consider that there may be."

Autumn looked confused.

> "I never heard any of those stories."

> "The man who sold me the house told me. I once had the chance to sit down and talk to him. He told me all kinds of ghost stories, considering how old he was I thought it was his imagination. After tonight, I think I believe him."

Autumn was glad in this case, if it hadn't been for Maggie she could have lost her brother, but he's safe now. Thanks to Maggie, now everyone was safe and peaceful. Noah and Logan took Autumn back home then went home themselves. It was quite a night, now everyone was safe and what was left of the night would be peaceful.

It was a long week, now the building for the orphanage was completed. Noah held a special ceremony for the opening, the entire town gathered round to help celebrate. Noah welcomed everyone.

> "I would like to welcome all of you and thank you for coming and being here today for the re-opening of the orphanage. So many things have happened since this building, many new beginnings. I would especially like to thank all who took part in rebuilding the orphanage. One of the new beginnings for the children. As I said there were other new beginnings, Tim Birescik has a new beginning, he married and has a new wife, beautiful new wife. There are other new beginnings but for now this is about the orphanage. At this time Tim would like to say a few words. Please welcome, Tim Birescik."

The crowed roared and clapped, it was a joyous occasion.

> "Thank you, all of you. As Noah said since we lost the original building not only is this building new but also the many other changes have taken place, happy ones. We owe a debt of gratitude to each of you, there isn't a person here who didn't take part one way or another to help these children. We thank you. One more thing before I step down. We have a new priest to take over the running of the orphanage. Will you please. help me welcome, Father Reuben."

Father Reuben stood up and thanked everyone, then prayed for the new building and to keep and protect the children. Everyone repeated Amen, then he cut the ribbon. Cheering began and the children were happy and jumping. They gathered around Father Reuben to get to know him better. Ronnie wished Arjun could have been there to see this all, he was a part of this. Father Reuben invited Autumn to come up and say a few words.

> "Thank you Father. I also would like to thank everyone who has taken a part in the new orphanage. I'm very happy to announce that the money we raised from the fair provided beds, blankets and sheets, anything the children need to start over. Your generosity brings great comfort to these children, thank you."

The celebration went on for about another hour, then everyone went back to their lives. Austin and Autumn went inside to visit with the children for a while and watch them play.

> "Austin, look how happy they are, isn't it wonderful?"

He smiled as they watched them run and play, to see their happy faces once more. "Austin, Austin. Are you all right?"

"I'm sorry, yes I'm fine."

"You have a strange look on your face."

"It's just so good to see them happy."

They didn't stay very much longer, Autumn had a saloon to run and Austin has his job. Sally ran up to Autumn as they were getting ready to leave.

"Miss Autumn, will I ever see you and Mr. Austin now we have a new home?"

Sally looked as though she would cry.

"Well of course you will, we'll still go on picnics and all different things like before."

Sally reached up to give her a hug and held so tight, Autumn almost had to pry her off.

"Why would you think that would change?"

Sally hung her head and shrugged her shoulders.

"Sally, why would you think that?"

"I just thought since we have a new home you don't have to see me anymore."

Autumn hugged her and held her, she never thought that would come up.

"Sally, I once told you I would never leave you. Remember?"

"Yes."

"Well I meant that, you will always be a part of my life. Okay?"

Sally shook her head and dried her tears away. Austin promised to take her for a ride to the lake the next day. She was so happy she would still see Autumn and Austin. They said so long for that day and would see her the next day.

"Autumn, you did a great job for those kids."

"It wasn't just me, people pitched in to build, donate, work a booth. Everyone was involved somehow."

"No, if it weren't for you planning the fair who would make donations, who would work a booth? It was your idea to put it all together, the reason those children have more than just a building. The money you raised provided beds, blankets, food, things they needed to rebuild their lives, and there was more left over to provide a play room on rainy days or snow days. You did more than you think. I'm really proud of you. I'm sure I'm not alone on that."

Autumn just smiled.

"Well I do need to get in there and get some work done. Will you stop by for supper? I'm making pot roast, potatoes beans and cornbread."

"Try and stop me."

He kissed her her cheek then was on his way. Autumn thought she would stop at the jailhouse to ask Noah if he would be over for supper. When she went inside she found him nearly doubled over and in pain, though he was trying to fight it was no secret.

"Oh God Noah what's wrong?"

"Not sure, think it's appendix."

That's all she needed to hear, she ran out the door and over to Logan's office.

"Logan come quick, it's Noah!"

"What's wrong?"

"He thinks it's his appendix, he's leaning over in his chair in pain."

Logan grabbed his bag and they went to the jailhouse. There was Noah just as Autumn had described. Logan rushed to his side to examine him, it is indeed his appendix.

"Autumn do you think you can help get him to my office?"

Noah cried out.

"No I just can't leave him here"

Logan knew that wouldn't work, there was only one thing left.

em>Jeanette Kossuth McAdoo

"All right not to the office, how about the back room on the cot?"

"Fine, I can do that."

"Autumn I need some things from my office, would you get him on the cot and make him comfortable? I'll be back in a flash."

Autumn helped him to get to the cot, she removed his boots from his feet and helped him to lay back. She was hurting almost as much as he was. It was difficult for her to see him in the pain he is in. Logan was back as quickly as he said.

"I'm going to have to remove your appendix right now, they are ready to burst."

Logan gave him a shot to sleep while he preforms surgery. Autumn was there to assist.

"Thank you for coming to get me, this isn't his first flare up, this was bound to happen. We both knew that."

Both Logan and Autumn were perspiring, Autumn never was a part of surgery before, at times she turned her head. Logan was known as the best doctor in Anaconda, people came from other towns just to see him. The minutes seemed to drag by, Autumn was praying for Noah and Logan.

"How is it going?"

"Great, I'm almost through."

She couldn't understand how he was able to suffer this long, Noah always was strong about things like this. Pain never seemed to bother him, much. At least now he'll be free of pain.

"That's it, we're done. He'll be fine now. I'll check in on him periodically and if he needs something for pain, I'll give him a spoonful of this. He should rest comfortably for the most part."

"I'd be happy to stop in and help take care of him, I know your schedule is busy. I can come back in an hour."

"Tell you what, I'll come back in thirty minutes, you stop in in an hour and we'll share the time. That way he'll have the total care he needs."

"That's fine, I'll be here late then."

She went back to the saloon leaving Logan with Noah. As she was walking in she noticed Ronnie sitting at a table with Victoria and Tim. Ronnie turned to joke with her.

> "And just where have you been young lady?"

> "I was at the jailhouse with Noah and Logan. I was assisting Logan with Noah's appendix, he had to have them removed."

> They all looked at her amazed at what happened. "What? Are you serious?"

> "Very, I stopped in to see if he would be over for supper. He was leaning over in his chair in pain so I ran and got Logan. He said he wasn't surprised that it was a matter of time. Apparently Noah has been having problems before."

Ronnie couldn't believe it, Noah never said a word to him about that.

> "I'm sorry I'm late."

Cora came out with supper for everyone.

> "I knew what you were planning for supper, I hope you don't mind I started cooking. When I looked outside I did see you running to Logan's office so I thought I would just finish what I started."

> "That's fine, I'm so glad you did. Thank you very much."

> "I heard what you said about Noah, I hope he'll be all right."

> "He will now, thank you for asking. I don't know what I would do without you and Victoria."

Just then Austin came in and joined them. Autumn went to fix a plate for him while Ronnie filled him in about Noah. Austin looked up at Autumn.

> "Well if that's the worst thing that could happen right now, I think we can handle that. We've had so much worse going on, of course I'm sure he will be fine with a doctor like Logan. It's a shame it had to happen at all."

Autumn was feeling much better about things right now, Austin was right about one thing. Noah could have died if his appendix had burst. Logan caught it in time.

"Oh look at the time, I promised Logan I would check on Noah, I'll be right back."

She rushed over to the jailhouse to see how Noah was doing, when she went to the back room he was awake.

"Noah, how are you feeling?"

"I'm fine, not much pain at all. Doctor Logan says I can't eat yet, even though I'm starving, but I can deal with that."

"Tell you what, I'll go bring you something from the saloon. I know what I can give you, I'll be right back."

As she was walking out the door Logan was coming inside.

"I thought you were here earlier?"

"I was but I want to make sure he doesn't try to talk you into bring him solid food."

"He didn't, I'm going to get him some broth. I'll be back. How about you, would you like some supper?"

"I was all ready at the saloon and had mine, I don't want to tempt Noah. Thank you though."

Autumn smiled and went on her way. Austin was waiting for her when she came back.

"Well hello stranger, I was hoping we could go out tonight. Logan said he was going to sit with Noah through the night. So what do you think, can we get together?"

"Sure, let me just take this to Noah and I'll be back."

She rushed the broth over to him, Logan told her he would take care of things while she went out with Austin. Both Logan and Noah told her to have a good time. When she walked in the saloon she told Austin she would change and be right back downstairs.

"No you don't you look fine the way you are, let's go."

He picked her up and carried her out to the buggy. She didn't know what to say. He hopped into the buggy and tugged at the reins, they were on their way.

"So could I ask where we're going?" "You'll find out when we get there."

Austin was being mysterious, and she was so curious she could bust. It appeared he was heading to the lake, until he made a turn. Now she was totally lost.

"Well, here we are."

She looked around, there is a view of the lake but she still didn't understand.

"Where are we?"

Austin laughed and hugged her close.

"What do you think about this area?"

She looked around, it is beautiful, she especially enjoyed the view of the lake but still she didn't understand.

"I can see you're still puzzled. I found out this piece of land is for sale. I'm thinking of buying it, so what do you think?"

"Austin, it's beautiful, are you really thinking of buying this?"

"More than just buying it, I want to buy it, build a home for us here and raise our children here."

Autumn had no words to speak, all she could do was stare at him.

"Staring isn't going to help me make a decision, I need to know how you feel bout this land."

"Did you say build a home for us and raise our children here?"

"That is what I said."

She took a deep breath and hugged him so tight, she couldn't let go.

"Austin, I think this would be wonderful."

"Well there is more. I also need to know how you would feel about adopting Sally and Liz. We can still have our own children, but they just seem to be a part of us."

Autumn fell to the ground in tears, she was so happy she couldn't believe he thought about adopting. She loved Sally very much and Liz. Austin sat next to her on the ground holding her in his arms.

> "You are an amazing man, I love you so very much. Yes Yes, I would love nothing better."

Chapter 8

Autumn closed the saloon for one day, she was having a special family supper with her brother Ronnie and her cousins Noah and Logan, and of course Austin. He wasn't family yet but he will be soon enough. She gave Victoria and Cora the day off and Autumn decorated the saloon for this occasion. Everything had to be perfect, and generally was when she set her mind to things that was important her. This certainly was.

She looked up and saw Austin walk in with Ronnie.

> "We stopped at Noah's house on the way over, he and Logan will be here in about five minutes. So what's the occasion?"

> "Never mind Ronnie, when everyone is together all of you will know."

She poured them both a drink while they were waiting, Autumn was so excited she thought she would bust. Noah and Logan arrived and Autumn poured them a drink, then they sat at the table, everyone was wondering what was going on. Autumn tapped her glass with a knife.

> "May I please have everyone's attention. This is a special supper today. Austin and I have wonderful news to tell you all."

Noah smiled and then he stood up.

> "Yes, we all ready know the two of you are going to be married."

Autumn and Austin smiled, then Austin took a turn to talk.

> "Yes we are, and yes that is old news. We do have some of the best news ever."

Autumn took his arm and smiled.

> "Austin bought some land near the lake, we're going to build a house and raise our children their."

Ronnie's eyes grew big.

"You're pregnant?"

"No of course not silly. After we're married, we are going to adopt Sally and Liz."

Everyone was speechless but very happy for them, all of them.

"Sally and Liz don't know yet, we need to check into the arrangements first, before we tell them. We don't want to get them excited then it can't happen. We couldn't put them through that."

They were all so happy and excited for all of them. The four of them would make the perfect family. Austin helped Autumn serve supper and they talked and talked about so much. The kind of house they would build, the girls, and a beautiful family they will be. As they finished Autumn announced she had a cake for this celebration. Just as she made the announcement two men walked in the saloon.

Autumn froze and gazed at them both, suddenly she let out a terrifying scream. Everyone looked at her wondering why.

"You're the two men who murdered our parents!"

Ronnie looked at her not knowing how she could know that.

"I was in the loft and when they came in the house I saw what they did, it was them."

Logan and Noah looked at each other but never spoke.

"Did ya hear that Amos? I told you I heard something that day."

Buck told him to be quiet.

"Now they know that for sure, they wouldn't have known a thing till you opened your mouth."

Ronnie stood up and spoke to them both.

"Why did you kill them? What did they do to you?"

The Bart brothers just looked at each other and laughed.

"Well now son it was an honest mistake. We were given the wrong information and the wrong names. So you see it really wasn't our fault."

Noah spoke up next.

"That's your excuse? It was a mistake? Taking a life is no mistake and there is no excuse for doing so."

Autumn was in tears and screamed at the brothers.

"You filthy beasts, what gives you the right?"

Buck just looked at her and asked her questions.

"Now for a nice looking woman like you that's dirty talk. You sure are a pretty one."

Ronnie punched him and Logan pulled him back, Autumn ran into the kitchen.

"Well now son that was a mistake, one your gonna have to pay for."

The brothers took one step back and drew their guns, two shots were fired. Buck and Amos fell to the floor. Noah knew he shot one, when he turned to see where the other shot came from, he saw Autumn standing there with a rifle. She couldn't move, just stood there staring at the brother's. Logan went over to her.

"Sweetheart, are you all right?"

He slowly took the rifle from her, then she let out a scream and went down on her knees crying.

"I remember, I wish I didn't but I do."

Ronnie walked over to her and held her tight in his arms. She couldn't stop crying, it were as though she relived the whole incident all over again. Ronnie looked up at Logan, Austin asked him if there were anything he could do for her.

"Right now I can sedate her, at least it would calm her down. Since she now remembers what happened, I don't know what kind of shape she will be in, all we can do is wait and be there for her. Logan ran to his office to get his bag, when he came bag he gave Autumn and injection. Soon she grew tired, Ronnie carried her upstairs and put her in bed. He sat with her waiting for her to wake up, he needed to be there for her.

This was not something he expected, he did want her to regain her memory but not at this expense. Noah came into the room and his hand on Ronnie's shoulder.

"It's the worst thing to remember, but at least now she can work on putting it all behind her now."

Ronnie nodded, he knew Noah spoke the truth, no matter how painful it is for her right now. Austin came in after Noah.

"If you like I can sit with her a while."

"Thank you Austin, but I really need to stay with her right now. You understand?"

"Of course, if there is anything I can help with..." "Sure, I'll let you know. Thanks"

Ronnie sat there with his sister, watching her and waiting for her to waken. Several hours had gone by, she was still sleeping. Night came along with a breeze. Ronnie opened the window to cool off some. He looked up in the sky as if her were searching for something.

"Mom, Dad...Autumn saw what happened and I never knew that. I'll take care of her and see her through this I promise. Me, Noah and Logan. I can't help but feel both of you will be there for her too. She needs us now more than before. Things are going well for her, she's getting married. You probably all ready know that. I'm good, but Autumn needs you now, please?"

Ronnie gazed at the stars one last time, then he turned towards Autumn, when he did he saw their parents. Their mother sitting on the bed and their father standing there stroking Autumns forehead. He couldn't speak he just stood there and watched. Finally he spoke.

"Mom, Dad?"

They looked up at him and smiled. Ronnie walked towards them and they turned to him.

"Sweetheart, we never left either of you. We're always here for you."

"Your mother's right. We see everything going on with both of you. When either of you really need us, we're close by."

They looked back at Autumn, blew her a kiss then they faded into the night. Autumn began to wake and Ronnie rushed to her side. She looked up at him.

"Ronnie, I know you won't believe me but I saw mom and dad."

"I believe you, they were here, I saw them too."

"Really you did? I could feel them here, I could feel a hand on my forehead stroking back and forth. My hand being held."

"Dad had his hand on your forehead and Mom was holding your hand. They said they would always be here for us, and they are watching over us. How are you feeling?"

"Honestly? I'm not sure. I still feel a little shaky."

She paused a moment and began to think, then tears came to her eyes.

"Oh my God, I can remember. I remember what happened. Those vultures."

Ronnie sat with her holding her to calm her.

"Why didn't you tell me you were in the loft?"

"I couldn't remember, not until today when they came back. They're here, they're dangerous, what are we going to do?"

"It's fine they can't hurt anyone ever again, I promise."

She looked at him terrified.

"How can you be so sure?"

"You and Noah shot them. They didn't survive. No one will be hurt by them ever."

Autumn sat up leaning back and gathering her thoughts. Then she remembered holding a shot gun and shooting. She breathed a sigh of relief.

"It's over, really over?"

"Yes it is."

There was a knock on the door. Autumn called for them to come inside. It was Austin.

> "Hey, I just thought I would give you a break Ronnie. I see Autumn woke up, how are you feeling?" Ronnie decided to give them some time together.

> "I'll talk you later, take care Autumn. I love you."

> "I love you too Ronnie."

He left closing the door behind him.

> "Well I'm not sure but it seems something happened?"

> "No nothing, I just got my memory back. I almost wish I hadn't, but I guess there's a reason for why I did."

> "You can't really move on if you hadn't remembered, now you can. Things will be fine, you'll see."

Autumn wrapped her arms around Austin's neck holding on to him. He pulled her arms away and helped her lay back down.

> "It's the middle of the night and you need your sleep. We can talk more in the morning."

He leaned over and kissed her then said good night. She closed her eyes and Austin sat in the chair to make sure she would be fine. Logan knocked on the door slowly opening to check in on Autumn. Austin motioned for him to come in, they talked.

> "I'm not asleep yet. Hey Logan."

> "So I just saw Ronnie and thought I would come over to check on you. How are feeling?"

Autumn told him she was feeling a little shaky but better.

> "I am still kind of tired."

> "Well that's to be expected, you've been through a lot."

He did a quick check on her to make sure everything was going well. He looked at Austin.

"She's going to be fine, she has her memory back. All that's ahead for her now is improvement."

Then he looked at Autumn.

"I do advise you close the saloon one more day, you do need your rest. One day won't hurt."

"Whatever you say doctor."

Autumn smiled, winked at Austin then went right back to sleep. Logan looked at Austin and asked him to step outside the room.

"I believe she'll be fine now. I'm not sure what happened but she really is showing improvement."

"To tell you the truth I'm not sure myself, but she does seem a heap better."

"I would just let her sleep, let her get up when she's ready. She's been through so much she could really use the rest."

"Anything you say. Thank you for coming over so late."

Logan shook his hand then went back home. Austin went downstairs, there was still a mess that needed cleaned up and he wasn't tired. He was restless and needed something to do.

The next day after breakfast Sally went to see Logan. She really wanted to see Autumn.

"Tell you what, let me finish this paper work it won't take long. Then I'll take you over, how does that sound?"

"All right! I sure do miss her."

Logan smiled, he knew how much Sally loved Autumn and she loved Sally.

"Well all done, are you ready?"

"Yes sir Mr. Logan, I'm ready."

Sally had a big smile on her face and was anxious to see Autumn. She held his hand and they walked over together. When they walked in they found Autumn and Austin having coffee at a table. Autumn's eyes grew big, she was as anxious to see Sally and Sally was to see her. Sally ran over to her and leaped into her arms.

"Miss Autumn, I missed you."

"I missed you too Sally."

Austin watched the two of them together and felt warm inside.

"Well ladies how would you to feel about a ride today? I think it would be good for all of us."

They both agreed, Logan was smiling and shaking his head. This would make a great picture. They looked like a family.

"I have another idea. Sally would you and Liza like to have supper with us?"

"Oh yes, we sure would!"

Autumn looked at Austin.

"We still have C A K E left, we can have that after supper."

Austin looked at Logan.

"What if we get together again for supper, with the kids and have a real celebration. Would you and Noah be able to join us?"

"Oh please Mr. Logan, please say yes?"

Logan smiled at Sally and picked her up in his arms.

"If that's what you want, we will be here."

Sally was so pleased she hugged him tight.

"Oh thank you, and thank you for taking care of Miss Autumn. I love her so much, I wish she could be my mommy."

Autumn and Austin looked at each other, it were as if she all ready knew.

"Autumn I will take care of everything, you stay in bed and rest and I'll give you enough time to get dressed. Sally, let's go talk to Father Reuben about you and Liza having supper with us tonight."

Logan sat with Autumn to talk for a while. About her memory coming back, how she was handling that.

> "I remember that horrid day now, at first I wish I hadn't but I think I can move forward now. I think it was good for me to remember."

> "You're going to be just fine, it was good and healthy for you. I'll leave you to rest up, you'll need your strength for later."

Logan hugged her then left. Autumn wanted to wear something special for supper. This would be extra special, the children would be there with, family together again and this time it would be a great time. After she picked out what she wanted to wear she laid them on the chair and climbed back into bed, she felt a little tired. A short nap may do her some good.

Austin was downstairs getting everything ready for that evening. Only this time he asked Victoria and Tim to come and Cora. They were close enough to be family, there was no way he could exclude them. They all have been through a lot together, he couldn't leave them out. It took Austin all until it was time for supper to get everything ready, then he went upstairs for Autumn.

> "Come in Austin."

> "How did you know it was me?"

> "Well it's supper time, and I'm ready. How do I look?"

She was always amazing to him.

> "You're stunning as always. I need to tell you something before you come down. I also asked Victoria and Tim and Cora to join us. I hope you approve."

The smile on her face told him she did approve.

> "Of course, they are family. We're lucky you know."

> "Yes we are, and blessed. May I?"

He held his arm for her to take carefully guiding her down the stairs, only half way down she stopped.

> "Oh Austin, it's all so beautiful. You really did all this?"

"I did have a little help from Cora and Victoria. I have no sense for decorating."

"Well I do love it and I appreciate it and of course all of you."

They came downstairs and everyone hugged Autumn letting her know they were so happy she is fine. They all sat down to eat, talk and enjoy each others company. Sally and Liz sat opposite of each other at the table but close to Autumn. They laughed, and sometimes even sang a little. Nothing was better than being together.

Austin stood up and asked for everyone's attention.

"So last night Autumn and I made an announcement, tonight we have Sally an Liz here so I would like to repeat everything if all of you don't mind."

All the attention was directed to Sally and Liz, only they had no idea what was going on or about to happen. Austin walked over to Autumn, he picked up Liz and she picked up Sally and sat the girls on their lap. Austin started the announcement.

Liz, Sally, last night we told most everyone here that Miss Autumn and I are getting married. We also told them we are going to build a home near the lake."

The girls looked at each other, a little disappointed. Then Autumn spoke.

"You both don't look very happy, is something wrong?"

Sally looked up with tears in her eyes.

"I guess that means we can't be together and do things anymore."

That was all it took for Liz to start crying. Then Autumn pulled out her handkerchief to wipe their eyes.

"No, that's not what it means. We still hope to see you both."

Then Liz asked her question.

"How can we? You won't be living here anymore?"

Austin smiled at them.

"Well...we were hoping after Miss Autumn and I were married, we could have your permission to adopt you, both. That would mean you would be our children and live with us?"

Their faces changed that quickly. Then Liz asked.

"You mean it, we would live with you? That means Sally and me would be sisters."

Autumn smiled and hugged the girls.

"That's right, you and Sally would be sisters and our children."

That was all good, until Sally's face dropped again. Austin saw her face.

"Sally, wouldn't you like that?"

"No I wouldn't, I would hate that."

She jumped off of Autumn's lap and ran upstairs. Autumn quickly chased after her.

"Sally...we thought you would like living with us and having Liz as a sister?"

"I don't want her to be my sister."

"I don't understand, I thought you liked her?"

"I do, she's my very best friend."

"Then what's wrong?"

Sally wiped her eyes hugging Autumn and trying her best not to cry.

"If she is going to be my sister, that means we can't be best friends. We promised we would always be best friends."

Autumn held her and rocked on the edge of the bed, stroking her hair and trying to calm her down.

"Sweetheart, that's not true. You can still be best friends. There are brothers and sisters who are best friends. Just because your related and live in the same house doesn't mean you can't be best friends. Ronnie is my brother and my best friend."

"Really? You mean it, for real?"

"Yes for real. Anyone can be a best friend, whether you're family, or not."

Sally was so happy she ran back downstairs to tell Liz. Autumn followed behind her and winked at Austin so he would know everything was fine. Sally was hugging Liz and told her they could still be best friends. Everyone was happy that night, including Sally and Liz, they are going to be a family. A real family with a mom and dad, a home and near the lake where they can go fishing. Everything is going to be wonderful. Autumn called to everyone for their attention.

"Now that we all know the news I still have a cake to celebrate."

Sally and Liz both looked at each other with big smiles.

"Oh boy, cake! Sally, I think we're really going to be happy."

"Yeah, Miss Autumn will be our mom and Mr. Austin will be our dad, and now cake too."

Everyone looked at the girls and were laughing, Autumn and Ronnie went to get the cake to bring out and serve.

"Ronnie I could have done this myself, you should be sitting out there."

"I know you could have, but I wanted a moment to check on you..."

"I'm fine now, really."

"Good, and to wish you well. We've been through quite a lot, now look at us. We survived it all, our dreams are coming true.'

"Yes, and mom and dad will always be with us."

He gave his sister a huge hug, they were going to be happy at last. Never thinking all their troubles would end.

"Just one thing Ronnie, I am so very sorry about Maggie."

"So am I, Arjun taught me to have peace with that. Like mom and dad, she too will live in my heart."

"Well we better get this cake out there."

Ronnie carried the cake and Autumn carried the plates and forks. The girls stood up and cheered clapping as hard as their little hands could. Tim stood up to say a few words.

"I would like to make a toast. Don't worry girls it won't take long. Victoria and I have been very happy together, so I know Austin, Autumn, Sally and Liz will be also. You're a fine looking family and if there is anything Victoria and I can do, please let us know. You both have done so much for us. Here's to you and your family, and to Ronnie and his new ranch. I've been out there and it is coming along very nicely. May we all be blessed and as happy as we are right now."

Liz looked at him and asked.

"Hey I thought it wasn't going to be long, we want cake."

Autumn cut the first two pieces for the girls. Austin played his harmonica and everyone laughed and danced, it was a very special celebration. Austin and Autumn were in a corner talking, when Cora saw them.

"Hey you two come out here and have some fun." Autumn was glowing.

"Well it looks like Austin and I have another announcement to make. He all ready spoke to Father Reuben, we're getting married at the end of this week."

"That's right, so I really have to work on getting our cabin built."

Everyone smiled and was so happy, the men all offered to pitch in and help. The women were talking about the wedding and making plans, Victoria and Cora wanted to plan and decorate for that. Autumn helped with Victoria's wedding. Victoria put her arm around Autumn.

"You did it for me, let me do this for you. Please?"

Autumn agreed only because there was so much that needed done. Then Cora asked her about her wedding dress.

"I have a dress, in the top of my closet is my mother's dress. I always had hoped to wear it someday. Now I will be."

The girls were sneaking another piece of cake when Logan caught them.

"Hold on you two, let me cut this for you. Both of you are too young to be using a knife."

"Thank you Mr. Logan."

"You know I just thought of something. You won't be calling me Mr. Logan anymore."

They had a sad look on their faces.

"Don't look sad it's not going to be bad. You both will be calling me Uncle Logan. We're going to be family, remember? Noah will be Uncle Noah."

The girls started jumping up and down, they were happier than before. Neither one of them thought about that. It was starting to get late and the girls had to go back to the orphanage. Austin and Autumn would walk them back. Autumn went over to let them know soon they would be leaving.

"Okay little ladies, right now you still live at the orphanage, so we have to take you back. Finish your cake and Austin and I will walk you over."

Noah and Logan pulled Autumn aside.

"You know things turned out very well I think, don't you agree Logan?"

"I sure do. We couldn't be happier for all of you. You will have your family, Ronnie has his ranch and Noah is now a sheriff. Things have changed so much since you and Ronnie moved here and all for the best."

"Thank you both so much, we made a good decision. Oh dear." Noah saw her face.

"Is something wrong?"

"One thing is missing. Marsha, if only she could be here this would be perfect."

Noah was sure he could get her here in time.

"That's no problem, you're getting married at the end of the week.
She'll be here, I promise."

Autumn thanked Noah, she knew he meant every word he spoke however he would manage. Austin walked over to Autumn and told her they had better take the girls back. The rest of the adults stayed and had their cake till the happy couple came back from the orphanage. Victoria and Cora started to clean up while the men sat and talked.

Noah pulled Logan aside to talk privately.

"I have a thought, I know some men who build log cabins, just like the one Autumn always dreamed about. What if I got them together, we can help and that could be our present to them. What do you think?"

"I think that's a great idea. Let's get out of here and talk."

Logan explained to everyone he and Noah had to leave for an important matter. They said good night to everyone and went on their way. Ronnie caught up with them before they left to far.

"Is something wrong?"

Noah said to Logan they should tell Ronnie, he is her brother. Logan couldn't agree more.

"Noah knows some men who build log cabins, he was thinking we could get together to have them build the cabin for them and it would be our present to them. What do you think?"

"That is a great idea, mind if I get in on this deal?"

"Of course not, you are her brother. I'll talk to my friend then I'll get back to you and Logan with the details."

It was settled, they would meet again when Noah collected all the details. They passed Austin and Autumn on the way out and explained they had to leave, congratulated them and would see them the next day. When Autumn and Austin walked in the saloon they were surprised, everything was cleaned up, they and Victoria, Tim and Cora all sat down for coffee and talked a while longer.

"This has been a wonderful party, Austin and I couldn't be happier, and everyone has been so sweet. We appreciate all of you and all you have done."

It was getting late, everyone said goodnight and left for home. Austin was the only one who stayed behind.

> "Well it would seem we have a little time to ourselves." "It certainly does seem that way."

Austin pulled her close to kiss her goodnight.

> "Well it is getting late, and I do have things to get done. There will be plenty of time for this once we are husband and wife."

> "That's right, besides I also have things to get done. See you tomorrow?"

> "Try and stop me."

He kissed her once more then said goodnight. Neither of them could be happier and they both were looking forward to being wed. Autumn always dreamed about having her own family, now she was getting a husband, a home and children all at once.

The next day Noah, Logan and Ronnie all got together about building the cabin, Noah had already spoke to Austin about it so Autumn would really be the one surprised. Austin gave them all the specifications, so they all went to start on the cabin. Meanwhile back at the saloon Autumn was showing her dress to Victoria and Cora. She tried it on in case it would need altered, but it fit her perfectly. What a beautiful bride she will be, the dress was simple yet elegant trimmed in just a hint of lace. Her mother, Kim, had made the dress herself.

> "Autumn, this dress is gorgeous. It's so perfect on you." "Cora's right, I've never seen a more beautiful dress."

Autumn couldn't stop admiring it, but she had to stop and put it away.

> "Well ladies we have plenty to do, we should get downstairs and get started."

Noah was up early to send a telegram to Marsha, he paid for her train ticket so she could be at the wedding. Marsha and Autumn grew close in such a short time, it wouldn't be much of a wedding without her. Victoria's husband, Tim, was helping the men with the cabin. She knew what he was up to but he swore her to secrecy.

The men kept busy building while he women were planning and working on he wedding plans. Autumn went out and bought Sally and Liz dresses for the wedding, as long as they would be family someday she thought she may as well start treating them like family. She bought both girls coral colored dresses but different styles. Everything seemed to be coming together.

Late afternoon the saloon was filled, not one empty seat. Word was out about Austin and Autumn getting hitched. The player piano was playing, everyone was talking and laughing, just having a good time. Autumn walked in from outside, everyone in the place stood up and clapped and congratulated her as she worked her way through the crowed. Someone even stood up and made a toast to Autumn and Austin. There wasn't one person who didn't cheer for them. Autumn thanked everyone for herself and Austin.

"Because of the upcoming celebration between Austin and me, I'm buying a round of drinks for everyone here."

The crowed all hung around for a while, ate some chili and drank more. Soon it was getting late and the crowed started to pick up and leave a few at a time but not without hugging Autumn and wishing her their best. The ladies were tired, it was the biggest crowed they ever had at one time. By the time Cora, Victoria and Autumn finished cleaning up they were exhausted.

"Good night Victoria, Cora if you could stay a couple more minutes I'd really like to talk to you. I promise not to keep you long."

"Of course, is something wrong?"

"No not at all. After Austin and I are married, I'll be moving out of my room upstairs. I thought, if you would like, you could move in if you would like. Naturally you would still be paid, but you could take that room rent free. You work so hard for me and I do appreciate everything you do, I thought it would help save you money instead of paying for the room you have now. How would you feel about that?"

Cora was thing, it would be nice to save some money and be that close to

"If you're sure about this, it is awfully generous of you."

"I'm sure, once I move out that room is all yours."

"I don't know how to thank you."

"Not even necessary, I really want to do this for you."

Cora hugged Autumn and thanked her again for her generosity.

"You're a hard worker, you need a break somewhere. Have a good night, I'll see you in the morning."

Cora went upstairs to turn in while Autumn locked up for the night then went to bed. The next day and for the rest of that week everyone was working on something, the men on the cabin and the women on the wedding. Austin and Autumn went to the orphanage to make the arrangements for the adoption, both of them and Sally and Liz were very excited. After their meeting they took the girls out for lunch, just the feel of family felt so right and so good. After lunch they went for a ride then back to Autumn's room to try on the dresses she bought the girls.

"Liz, look! They are the prettiest dresses I ever saw!"

Liz looked at the dresses they had on, tears began to fill her eyes. Autumn noticed and sat down with Liz.

"Liz, sweetheart is something wrong?"

"I never had anything so pretty before, is it really mine to keep?"

Autumn smiled and hugged her, then dried her eyes.

"Of course you can keep it, and Sally too."

Sally ran over to Autumn and hugged her as tight as she could. Then Sally looked up at Autumn.

"You and Mr. Austin will really be our mom and dad, for real?"

"Listen you two, we are going to be a family. All of us. So yes, we will be your mom and dad. We want you girls to be happy and have a good life, we believe we can give you that and we want to give you that."

The two girls smiled like never before, they were so happy and anxious to have a mom and dad. Then suddenly Liz's face turned sad.

"Liz, sweetheart what's wrong?"

"Don't people give you presents when you get married?"

Autumn hesitated for a moment.

"Well yes, they do. Why?"

"Me and Sally can't buy you and Mr. Austin anything." "Hey, she's right. We can't."

Before both girls were in tears Autumn tried to explain things to them.

"Don't you girls know both of you are our present. The best present we could ever receive. You will be our children, and that is the best present anyone could ever receive."

Smiles came back to both of their faces.

"Hey, I have an idea. Before we take you back how about a big piece of pie. Victoria baked some for today."

"Really? Oh yes, please."

Autumn told the girls to wash their hands and face and she would take them downstairs and cut them a big piece of pie. They went downstairs and Autumn cut them a big piece just as she had promised the girls. She stood there watching them with Cora and Victoria by her side. Victoria pulled her aside.

"I have to say, I think you are going to be a great mom and Austin will be a great dad."

Cora joined in on the conversation.

"She's right, those girls love you both so very much."

Autumn smiled, she was so happy herself.

"We love them too, I hope you're right. I want to be a good mother to them. I have to admit I am nervous a bit."

"There's nothing for you to be nervous about. Cora and I see you with them all the time and you do great."

The girls had finished their pie and showed them a clean plate.

"Okay girls it's time to leave. We all need our sleep."

Victoria and Cora said goodnight to the girls and gave them a hug. Sally and Liz waived good bye as Autumn walked them out the door.

"I'll see you when I get back"

It was getting a little chilly out, Autumn gave her wrap to the girls and they shared it together. All she could think about was how adorable Sally and Liz are, and how happy they will all be together. Father Reuben met them at the door, Autumn walked them up the steps and the girls gave her back her wrap. They kissed and hugged each other goodnight, then went inside to get ready for bed.

"Sleep well you two."

"We will, goodnight mom."

Mom, wow it sounded so great. She felt a little tingly inside and warm. Autumn couldn't wait herself for them all to be a family. When she turned to walk back there was Austin standing there just staring.

"Mom huh? I'll bet that felt good."

"How long were you standing there?"

"Not long, I just got here. I was hoping to walk you home. I saw you leaving with girls."

"Well thank you very much kind sir, I would love for you to walk me home."

They both giggled, he stared at Autumn, she was glowing almost as much as the moon at night. It made him feel good to know how happy she seems to be, and how happy he intends to make her.

"Well here we are, will I see you tomorrow?"

"You will, I'll be stopping in for lunch. I have a lot of work to get done but seeings how I do have to eat I may as well eat in a place where I can see my wife to be."

"I do love you."

"I love you too, now off to bed. We all need our sleep."

He kissed her good night and made sure she made it inside safely. After Autumn reached her room she looked out the window and watched as Austin walked away. Then she sat in her chair for a bit dreaming about what her new life will be like. She is going to be a wife and a mother, all she wants now is to be a good one. As good as her mother was to her and Ronnie and a wife to their father. Her eyes grew heavy, it was time to turn in for the night.

The next morning Autumn was up early so she thought Austin might like some breakfast. She fixed a basket of muffins and some coffee and walked them over to his place. She knocked on the door but there was no answer. When she turned the knob the door was not locked, she went inside calling to him so she wouldn't startle him. Autumn set the basket on his desk, his bed was never slept in but there were no signs of anything being wrong outside of the fact he was missing.

"Autumn, stay calm. He's fine and maybe left earlier for work."

She picked up the basket and walked over to the stables, his horse was gone. Where could he be? She went to the jailhouse to see Noah. Rushing in through the door her eyes filled with tears Noah stood up and held her in his arms to calm her.

"Easy, calm down and tell me what happened."

She couldn't stop crying, she was ready to become hysterical.

"He's gone Noah he's gone. I went to the stable and his horse is gone."

"Who is gone?"

"Austin, I packed him some muffins for breakfast and took them to his place, when I got there I knocked but he didn't answer, the door wasn't locked so I went inside. His bed was never slept in, that's when I went to the stables and found his horse is also gone. Where can he be?"

"I wish I could tell you, did you find a note?"

"No, nothing."

She was so scared Autumn couldn't stop crying.

"Where can he be? He told me last night he was going home and going to bed."

Ronnie had walked in and saw her in tears.

"What's going on?"

Noah pulled him aside to talk, he told Ronnie everything Autumn told him. Ronnie went to his sister and took her hand.

"Don't worry, Noah and I will go out searching for him. We'll find him."

196

Ronnie walked her home and told her to stay put, he and Noah will bring him back. After he left her he and Noah went to get their horses to go searching for him. Logan was crossing the road when he saw them.

"So where are you two going?"

Ronnie and Noah filled him in on what was going on.

"This isn't good, and for sure there was no note?"

Noah shook his head.

"She said she was in his room and his bed was not slept in and not a note to be found anywhere."

"If I could I would go with you both." Ronnie knew he would.

"It's probably best, she may need someone and your the only other family member here. I sure would appreciate if you looked in on her from time to time."

"That I can do. Good luck, hope you can find him."

Logan thought he would stop up to see Autumn, maybe he could help calm her down. He went into the saloon and went up to see her, knocked on the door. She opened it, her eyes still filled with tears.

"I ran into Ronnie and Noah, they told me what happened." "What if he changed his mind and couldn't tell me, he just ran off?"

"I don't believe that anymore than I'm sure you don't. They will find him and bring him back, then you'll see for yourself."

"Do you really believe that?"

"Well of course I do. He loves you, the whole town knows that. He'll be back with Noah and Ronnie then you'll have forgotten he was even gone."

Autumn had a small smile on her face, trying her best and hoping Logan was right.

"I hope so, I love him like no other. I want to make him happy and be the best wife I know how."

"He feels the same way. He would never leave you, you mean too much to him. Believe me he will be back. I have to go right now but I'll come back to check on you. Lay down and try to relax, it will be fine."

Logan kissed her forehead, smiled and went on his way. As he was going back downstairs Victoria and Cora were waiting to hear about Autumn.

"She'll be fine once Ronnie and Noah find him. I'm sure it's nothing to be concerned about. It's just nerves."

They were sure he was right, she was a little anxious about things. When Logan left he heard the train pulling in, when it stopped he saw Marsha getting off.

"Marsha, you made it, everyone will be so glad to see you." "Thank you, so Autumn is getting married?"

Logan walked with Marsha long enough to fill her in about Austin being missing.

"The wedding is he day after tomorrow, he probably has nervous jitters himself. Everything will be fine, I'm sure of this."

"You know, seeing you could really help take her mind off things. Would you mind stopping over to see her?"

"Anything for her, I'll take care of that don't you worry."

Marsha went to check into the hotel then went over to see Autumn. Victoria and Cora were so happy to see her, they told her about Autumn. Marsha explained she all ready knew, that's why she was there. As she climbed the stairs Marsha gathered her thoughts to be prepared to talk to Autumn. When she reached her door, Marsha took a deep breath then knocked.

"Please go away, I want to be alone."

Again she knocked. This time Autumn opened the door.

"I said I want...Marsha!"

She hugged her tight and pulled her inside. They sat down and talked and soon Autumn was feeling better, but still worried.

"You know I think we should go shopping. Let's go."

"Shopping? At a time like this?"

"Especially at a time like this. It will take your mind off things for a
spell. Remember your getting hitched in a couple of days. Get your
things and let's go."

Autumn did as Marsha had asked her to, they went downstairs but Autumn checked with the girls to make sure they would be all right. Cora hugged her.

"Well of course we will. You and Marsha go enjoy yourselves and
don't worry about things here. Go on."

Marsha took a hold of Autumn's arm and walked out of the saloon. First they went to the dress shop, there were many pretty dresses. Surely Autumn could find something.

"How about this turquoise one, I think it would look great on you.
Look at this, a matching handbag with pearls."

That seemed to help some, Autumn was taken by the beauty of the dress and matching handbag. She loved pearls and turquoise was just stunning. They were at the shop at least a couple of hours. Time was going by and Autumn was kept busy, just what she needed. Marsha had found a couple of things herself. When they went to the register to pay for their items the lady made a comment about how she and Austin would make the perfect couple. Marsha motioned for the lady to not say anything, but it was too late. They paid for their merchandise then left the store.

"After Marsha what if he put just changed his mind, or what if he's
hurt somewhere?"

"Now you listen to me, Austin is a big boy and very capable of taking
care of himself. You know as well as I do he's a very resourceful man,
if he does need help he will find a way. That man loves you more than
you know and he would never think of leaving you. Deep down you
know that, you have to hold on to faith. You will see him again, he
will be back."

Autumn stood there letting everything she told her sink in, she was right. The entire town could see what they have together. All he's done, of course he just wouldn't leave like that.

"You're right, I'm sorry. I guess I just let the best, or the worst get to
me. Austin always told me I have to believe and hold faith in people.
That means him too, so that's exactly what I'm going to do."

"Good girl, now let's have some lunch, I'm famished."

"Let's go back to the saloon I'm sure they have something ready."

"Oh no, we're going to the hotel, I'm buying."

Autumn was feeling better all ready, they went up the street to go to the hotel when they saw Ronnie and Noah riding into town. Autumn looked at them hoping for an answer.

"We didn't find anything yet, Ronnie and I came back for lunch then we'll head back out."

Just as they dismounted their horses and empty horse came into town and straight over to Autumn.

"Oh my God, it's Austin's horse. Look, there's a note."

Noah detached the note that was on the saddle bag. Austin was hurt, he needed help.

"Ronnie go get Logan and tell him to bring his bag. I'll meet you both at the Anaconda Range, tell him to hurry."

Autumn had a frightened look on her face, Noah knew she was scared out of her mind.

"Don't worry, it's not that bad really."

"Is that so, then why do you need Logan?"

"Sweetheart listen to me. Austin hurt his leg so he will need medical attention, but it can't be that bad, if it were he wouldn't have been able to get this note to us. Relax he will be fine. Don't worry. We'll all see you when we get back."

Noah jumped on his horse and went as fast as he could, Logan, Ronnie and Tim were right behind him with his wagon.

"Autumn, you know what he said is true. If he were really bad he couldn't have sent this message to us."

"All right, I'll try to be calm, you're all right. I'll be fine. Come on let's go have lunch."

Autumn did her best to put on a brave front until she could see Austin for herself. When they walked in the hotel and sat down they ordered lunch, Marsha wanted to hear more about the wedding. Anything to keep Autumn's mind off of Austin.

"Well I have my mother's dress, she made it herself. It's beautiful, I can't wait to show it to you. Just a small ceremony nothing fancy."

"Sounds very romantic."

"Yes, and we're adopting Sally and Liz after we become husband and wife. Austin bought some land near the lake and he's building a cabin for us to live in, it's all going to be wonderful."

"Yes it will be, and you'll be a great mother and wife."

"I hope so, thank you."

They enjoyed their lunch and talked more about what was happening in each others lives. Autumn was so pleased that Marsha could make it, she told her it wouldn't be much of a celebration without her being there. They drank their coffee, Marsha paid the bill then they went back to Autumn's room so she could show Marsha her dress.

"Autumn, it's more beautiful than you told me. Your mother was very talented."

"She was, she really had a flair for dressmaking. My mother can't be there in person, but she will be there to see us. So will my dad."

That was the way Marsha wanted to hear her talk. Now she was sounding so much better. They heard Logan's wagon coming in, Autumn looked out the window. Austin was in the back with Logan. She ran downstairs and over to his office. Noah, Ronnie and Tim carried him inside and laid him on the table. Autumn rushed to his side.

"Don't worry it's not as bad as it looks, I'm fine really."

"I didn't know what to think or where you were, I was frightened."

Everyone stood there watching them, until Marsha told them they should leave them alone for a few moments, they closed the door and waited in the next room.

"I'm sorry, honest I am. I just couldn't sleep so I went for a ride to the Anaconda Range. An old tree fell on my leg, I was trapped under it, when I worked it out from underneath I was able to write that note and send Cocoa back with it, I knew he would come here. Logan said I'll be fine it's not serious, I may limp for a while but that's all."

"I thought you changed your mind about us and ran off."

"Darling, I could never change my mind about you. I've been looking for you all my life, you're not getting away that easy."

Autumn leaned over to kiss him, Austin held her tight as if he would never let her go.

"Well I better let Logan come in and tend to your leg. I'll see you later. I love you so much."

"I love you too and don't you forget that."

She smiled and left the room, Logan went in to tend to his leg. She couldn't thank Tim, Ronnie, Noah and Logan enough. Noah hugged her.

"Didn't I tell you things would be fine? Maybe next time you'll believe me."

She giggled and nodded yes, tears of joy were streaming down her face. Marsha took Autumn by her shoulders and they left to get things ready for their big day. Once again the women were tending to the decorations and Ronnie went back to his ranch to get things ready for the party after.

Austin asked Noah how the cabin was coming along. He said with all the help they had working on it, it will be ready for their special night.

"There are men out there now working on it as we speak."

"I hope she'll like it, I want her to be happy in our home."

"Trust me she will love it, it will be yours and hers and your two beautiful girls. That's what she really wants. You're giving her everything she's ever wanted."

Logan agreed, she is so happy she could bust wide open he told Austin.

"Now, you two are getting hitched the day after tomorrow so for now I suggest you stay off of your leg, give it a rest."

"Logan's right, I'm sure nurse Autumn will be over to take care of you."

They all laughed, they knew how she is and knew that was the truth. Autumn wasn't happy unless she could help someone. When Logan finished Noah and Tim helped him back to his room and saw he was comfortable.

"I'm sure Autumn will be by soon. Until then you rest. My brother's orders."

Tim smiled.

"I'll let her know you're home." "Thanks, both of you. All of you."

As Tim and Noah were leaving Autumn was on her way in.

"I thought he could use a hot meal. I made chili. Victoria has some waiting for you, go eat. I'm sure you're hungry."

Tim and Noah thanked her and went over to the saloon. Autumn knocked on the door before she went inside.

"I brought you some chili, I thought you could use a hot meal." "Well thank you, I am hungry and your chili is the best."

She sat with him while he ate and they talked, she was happy and nervous a bit about the wedding. Nothing would stop Austin from making her his wife.

"We'll be so happy together, I just know we will Austin."

"I do believe we will. I'm not worried at all."

"Well I do have things to do so I'll come back later for the tray. Rest easy. I love you."

Autumn closed the door behind her and rejoined the women to get things ready. Everything was back to normal, the women working on their things and the men finishing up what they needed to get done. The next day was nothing but hustling, from the time they woke up till nearly night. Father Reuben brought Sally and Liz over to the church to see Autumn.

"There she is, mom."

Autumn turned and saw the girls running to her.

"Look what we made, a present for you and our new dad."

Sally was so excited and so was Liz.

"Sally and me made this picture of all of us, a present for you and dad."

Autumn took the picture and raved about it, they put so much time into this drawing.

"You know what, this is our first family picture, I'm going to put it in a frame and hang it in our new home when it's done."

The girls were so excited.

"Thank you Father for bringing them over."

"They were so anxious to give this to you, they couldn't wait."

"Girls, thank Father Reuben for bringing you here. Now I don't want to say this but you have to go back with him. We're very busy here and there's nothing for you to do, but I really appreciate this, and so will Austin."

Autumn hugged the girls and Father walked them back to the orphanage. The women worked most of the day getting things ready for tomorrow. Ronnie walked in the church, he looked around and saw how beautifully they decorated.

"Ladies, you out did yourselves. Everything looks great. I'm here to invite all of you out to the ranch, I'm barbecuing, I think all of us have earned a rest and a little fun before the big day. Everyone be at the ranch at six, see you all then."

Ronnie walked over to Autumn to talk with her.

"I know you'll want to spend some time with Austin, so I'll have some food for you to take to him for both of you. Stop at the ranch half an hour early an I'll have it ready."

"Thank you Ronnie, that's very sweet. I'll see you then."

Ronnie left and Autumn stood there taking everything in, it couldn't have been more perfect.

"Well ladies, I can't thank you enough. This means so much to Austin and me. Of course we both look forward to seeing all of you tomorrow. Thank you again."

After all the work at the church was done everyone left to get ready to go to the ranch. Autumn was anxious to see Austin once more before their big day. Logan and Noah stopped in to see her.

"Well cousin, tomorrow is the big day. Noah and I are so happy for you both."

Noah offered his best to them as well.

"So we'll we see you at the ranch later?"

"No you won't, sorry. Ronnie told me to come out half an hour earlier. He's making a basket for Austin and me since he has to rest." Logan smiled and was pleased he was following doctors orders.

"Well then I suppose we'll see you tomorrow. Say hey to Austin for us and tell him take care."

"I will, thank you both very much."

Autumn stopped in to check on Austin, she knocked on the door and he told her to come inside.

"How did you know it was me?"

"No one knocks the way you do, how is everything at the church?" Everything looks so perfect, but..."

There was a look on her face and it wasn't a happy one.

"But what?"

"Well, are you sure you can go through with this tomorrow? I mean with your leg and the shape it's in?"

He couldn't help but smile at her, she was so concerned about him.

"Let me tell you something Miss Snyder, there is nothing on this earth that's going to keep me from becoming your husband tomorrow. Not one thing, I want us to be tied together for the rest of our lives. Is that clear?"

She smiled at him then sat next to him and hugged him so tight, he was so in love with her he could barely breath. Not that he minded, he was so in love with her he cold barely see straight.

"Ronnie is having a barbecue in a couple of hours. He told me to come out a half hour earlier that he would pack a basket for us. He didn't want to exclude you and he knows your restricted to your bed, so he's sending food for us."

"That was thoughtful of him to do that, but not necessary."

"I know, but why look a gift horse in the mouth? After all you will be his brother in law." Austin thought a moment and tilted his head.

"Funny how I never thought of that before, but you're right. In that case let him send all the food he wants."

The two of them sat and laughed for a few minutes, then she had to leave.

"Well time does go by quickly, I have to get ready and go pick up the food and I'll be back as soon as I can. Is there anything I can do or get for you before I leave?"

"No I'll be fine, just hurry back. I miss you all ready."

"I promise."

She blew him a kiss then left and closed the door. Autumn went back to her room to clean up and change. All she could think about was how lucky she is to have found someone so special. Her green dress is his favorite, so that will be the one she wears. This will be their last night being single, tomorrow they will be united as one. Autumn had his picture on her dresser and she gazed at his face.

"I never thought I could find true happiness as my mother did in a man, but I was lucky enough to find you, blessed even. I'll do my best to make you a good wife."

She kissed his picture then left to go to the ranch. As she went downstairs she asked Victoria and Cora how she looked, by the time she was half way down she realized they were closed today. Autumn was so used to them being there, it slipped her mind they were home getting ready to go to the ranch also. Checking around to make sure she was locked up, as she left she locked the front door then headed to the stables to pick up her buggy. When she was leaving she noticed Austin gazing at her from his window, Autumn waved to him.

It's a beautiful evening, not too hot and the sky painted beautiful colors of purple and pink. Ronnie's barbecue should be a success. Soon Autumn was riding into his ranch, briefly she stopped and stared.

"Oh my, what a marvelous job he did."

She said out loud then moved on. You could smell the meat cooking, it was peaceful and a time no one will soon forget. What a picture this site would make. When she pulled up closer to the ranch she saw Arjun and an Indian woman. Arjun helped her down from the buggy.

"Is good to see you again, this is my sister, Chandra."

She nodded to Autumn.

"Hello, I've heard a great deal about you. It was your brother who saved me, and I am grateful to him."

Autumn smiled at her.

"Yes, he told me. I'm so glad he was around to help you, I'm glad to see you're well. Welcome to his ranch, it's a pleasure to meet you."

Ronnie came out of the house with a basket.

"I saw you coming when I looked out the window. Here is the basket I promised you."

"Thank you Ronnie, we do appreciate this, you didn't have to go to all this trouble."

"No trouble, I know he has to rest and I didn't want either of you to miss out. I see you met Chandra?"

"Yes I did, she's a delightful person and very attractive."

Chandra smiled and bowed her head.

"Chandra told Autumn you are getting married tomorrow.

I made this bracelet for you, it's a bracelet made for any woman of the tribe who shall be married. It's meaning is a long and happy life together."

Autumn looked at the bracelet, the beauty of her work.

"Thank you so much, this means a great deal to me, I'll wear it tomorrow. Thank you. Well I should be going, it was wonderful seeing, and meeting you. I hope you will stay for our wedding, we really would love to have you there?"

Arjun looked at his sister, she nodded.

"We would be honored, thank you."

"I'm so glad, you're like family to us. Well have fun everyone, we'll see you tomorrow."

Ronnie hugged and kissed Autumn wishing her the best.

"You will make a beautiful bride and wife and mother." "Thank you Ronnie."

He helped her into the buggy then she waved to them and was on her way back to Austin. As she was leaving Tim and Victoria passed her waving to each other. This time Autumn was in a bit of a hurry to get to Austin before the food turned cold. The ride wasn't very long and she pulled the buggy up behind his building and went in the back way. She knocked on the door and heard Austin ask who was there.

"It's Autumn."

"Come in, I've been waiting for you."

She walked in and he was sitting in bed resting dressed in his best as she was. He couldn't take his eyes off of her.

"You're wearing the green dress I like so much!"

"I know it's your favorite, you're quite handsome yourself."

She walked over to his bed and set the basket down.

"I hope you're hungry, judging from the weight of this basket Ronnie packed a lot of food for us."

"What, no kiss first?"

Autumn fell into his arms and kissed him, he held her so tight. Then he looked at her.

"We are going to be so happy together, I know that."

"I think so too. Well let's see what Ronnie packed for us."

She opened the basket and found a box with a note from her brother. The note read:

I made this for mom and dad for their anniversary, now I want you and Austin to have this. My blessing to the both of you. Love Ronnie.

"Oh Austin, my brother carved this cross for our parents. Read the note."

Austin took the note and read it, then he looked at the cross.

"What craftsmanship, he did a great job on this.

He could make these and sell them. He really did a great job."

"We told him that, but he said then it would turn into work that would take the enjoyment out of what he does to relax. I can't believe he didn't keep this for himself."

She set the cross aside and they feasted on what he had packed for them. They talked over plans and talked about Sally and Liz and their new home. It was all exciting. After they ate she lay in his arms and they gazed out the window.

"Austin I can't wait for tomorrow, we will be husband and wife."

"I can't wait either, it's getting late. You should get back home and get some rest, big day tomorrow. I'll meet you at the alter."

He kissed her once more then sent her on her way. She pulled her buggy into the stable then started to walk home. When she looked into the sky there was almost a full moon, still beautiful.

"Mom, dad, I know you will be there tomorrow. I love you both very much."

Then she went into the saloon, locked the door and upstairs. Autumn changed her clothes then climbed into bed with the biggest smile on her face not knowing how she would get any sleep. When she closed her eyes and started thinking about her new life with Austin, she drifted into a deep sleep.

The next morning the sun was shining, Victoria and Cora went to Autumn's room to help her get ready, she was so nervous she couldn't remember their names. They all had a good laugh but did their best to calm her. Victoria looked at Autumn.

"Being a new bride, kind of, myself. You'll be fine. There's really nothing to be nervous about. The church is decorated, Austin will be waiting for you at the alter and you are a very beautiful bride."

"She's right, take some deep breaths, you'll be fine." Autumn listened to them and took a few deep breaths.

"Oh no, Sally and Liz. I have to go get them."

Cora and Victoria looked at each other then Cora offered to go get them.

"Relax, I'll go pick them up and we'll have them dressed and ready in no time. Now relax."

Cora rushed out the door while Victoria stayed to finish helping Autumn get ready.

"Autumn, everything will be great and you and Austin will be so happy. Tim and I are very happy. Just relax, everything will go smoothly, you will be surprised."

"I just want to be a good wife and mother."

"I've seen you with the kids and Austin, believe me you will be a great wife and mother. They all adore you and I see how you care for them, the entire town can see that. You have nothing to worry about."

Cora came back with the Sally and Liz, they barely recognized Autumn. She was so beautiful in her wedding dress. Liz went over to her.

"Will we look that pretty?"

"Well of course you both will. Now let's get you two dressed. We have to get to the church."

With three women helping the girls were dressed and ready to go, Victoria and Cora smiled till they were nearly in tears.

"Hey you two, no tears. It's too soon."

Everyone was dressed and ready, they left to go to the church holding onto Sally and Liz so they wouldn't get dirty. Victoria rushed over to make sure they were ready.

Standing there was Austin at the alter, Logan, and Noah up front. Victoria motioned to Cora, they were ready. Cora hugged Autumn then walked the children inside. When everyone was seated Marsha was playing the organ letting Autumn know to begin. One more deep breath and Autumn walked in, Ronnie stepped to her side to walk her down the aisle. It was all Autumn could do to keep the tears from filling her eyes.

Austin looked so handsome and waited patiently for Autumn to reach him. Autumn saw Chandra next to her as she walked down the aisle and showed her she was wearing the bracelet Chandra made for her. Then she whispered to Ronnie just before he gave Austin her hand.

"Thank you for the cross, it's perfect."

Ronnie kissed her cheek and said, you're welcome. The church was beautiful, decorated in coral streamers and lots of flowers. So many flowers the fragrance from them filled the church. Austin took her hand then they faced the priest to say their vows. Sally and Liz sat in the front with Marsha, Cora and Victoria, when Sally cried out.

"That's our new mom and dad."

She was very proud of that and everyone in the church giggled. Marsha explained they need to relax, they are about to say their vows. Still she and Liz had smiles on their faces and were as anxious as anyone. The priest welcomed everyone for coming before he began the ceremony.

This is the beginning of a new life, not only for Autumn and Austin but the children as well. Ronnie was happy Autumn could finally move on with her life now, she finally put the past to rest. Ronnie now has his ranch, Noah is now the sheriff of the town, and Logan is still a successful doctor everyone trusted, some people from just outside of town came to him. Things were finally looking up.

After they made their vows to each other Logan and Noah stood up to make an announcement.

"It doesn't seem all that long ago when Ronnie and Autumn moved here to Anaconda to be with us. Yes it was under unfortunate circumstances but I think things are getting better for them both, wouldn't you say Logan?"

"I have to agree, Ronnie and Autumn. We've always had some great times together and I'm sure as adults we will have more. We love you both very much. Austin, we welcome you into our family, as well as Sally and Liz. Noah and I wish all of you much happiness and love in your new lives together."

People clapped and cheered wishing them the best. Then Ronnie stood up.

"Thank you Noah and Logan and thank all of you for being here for this celebration. Now I would like to invite all of you, Father Reuben also of course, out to my ranch for a party, food and music. This is a time to enjoy. Please, you're all welcome. Autumn and Austin, congratulations we'll be waiting for you there to cut the cake, right Sally and Liz?"

"Oh boy, yes."

Sally and Liz rode with Autumn and Austin in the buggy then everyone else followed. It was a train of buggies going to the ranch, and Autumn was finally in tears. Austin gave her his handkerchief to dry her eyes with. Liz asked a question.

"Is it okay to call you mom and dad now?"

Austin had to explain to her they weren't really their parents just yet.

"I suppose there would be no harm in that but we're not your parents just yet, we do have to go and sign papers."

"Austin's right. We will be a family soon."

When they reached the ranch they were surprised to see a banner Ronnie put up. Welcome Mr and Mrs McAvoy. It was underneath the sign with the name of his ranch, "Aces High". The barn doors were open where the tables and chairs were set up and the cake on a table by itself. Another table filled with food. Ronnie caught up with them and he and Logan and Noah got together on a platform, Ronnie welcomed the new couple and invited everyone to dance. Autumn and Austin started it off with Sally and Liz with them, soon everyone joined in. Autumn looked up and saw a rainbow. She pointed it out to Austin.

"That's a present from my parents, they are wishing us well."

They both smiled and danced with Sally and Liz. It really is a new beginning for everyone.

COWBOY CHILI

1 can black beans, drained

2 green chili peppers, diced

1 Tbls olive oil

1 lb sirloin or round steak cubed

½ c chopped green pepper

½ c chopped onion

1 tsp cumin

1 tsp garlic minced

¼ tsp ground red pepper

1 Tbls flour

1 ¾ c beef broth

1 can (14.5 oz) diced tomatoes

1 Tbsp chili powder shredded cheddar

Brown beef in oil, add green pepper and onions. Add remaining ingredients except the flour. Cook and bring to a boil. Add the flour and turn down the heat. Simmer till thickened. Top with cheddar and serve.

Printed in the United States
By Bookmasters